Remember Me

Molly Brogan

Remember Me

By Molly Brogan

Remember Me Published By Molly Brogan Enterprises, Inc

Copyright © 2004 by Molly Brogan

ISBN: 978 0 6151 3811 4

Cover Design by Molly Brogan

Printed in the United States of America

Deepest gratitude to everyone that reads and recommends this book.

Remember me
Near the long day's end
When moonlight
Initiates your heart
To the journey of your soul.

Remember me clearly
As I stand, paused,
Listening for your soft entreat,
Waiting to offer a touch of kindness,
Understanding what you have to offer,
your mind, emotion and being.

As our spirits fly
In parting dance
I will wrap you in comfort
And keep you close
Until you next
Remember me.

Frankenstein

"Frankenstein, Frankenstein, Frankenstein....you look like Frankenstein."

The chant was coming from all three of her brothers. Little Mary was devastated. She wasn't old enough to understand that it was just a ploy to drive her away from their clubhouse. Nor could she fathom the rivalries between boys and girls in a family. She only understood that she was left without a playmate while her brothers seemed to be having fun together.

She screamed and ran upstairs as fast as her little legs would carry her. She could feel her little chest tighten as her breathing became more difficult. Sitting down in front of a mirror in her parents room she wondered what was so bad about "Frankenstein." Her brother's made it sound so bad, but the only place she had heard about Frankenstein was from her brothers. What did a Frankenstein look like? She studied her reflection in the mirror. She must be really ugly if they did not want to look at her or play with her. It was hard to see her face in the mirror through all the tears. She felt really sad. Her tears and wheezes got worse.

Then, out of the corner of her eye she spotted her cork! She had been searching for it for days, and here it was in her mother's drawer that had been left open a crack! Relief flooded her tiny body as she climbed up on an overstuffed chair and snatched her beloved cork. That familiar taste soothed her and her breathing came more easily as she sucked voraciously on the pacifier. She laid down in the chair and let the world fall away. A low, peaceful hum could be heard in rhythm with the cork moving in her mouth as she drifted into dream.

Brother's Brawl

She could hear herself screaming and knew that her body was shaking uncontrollably. The scene before her blurred and spun until she did not know where she was. After her mother broke up the fist fight between her brothers, her father took over and kept them apart. Her mother then turned her attention to Mary.

"Meg, get a glass of water," she told her sister as she wiped the tears from Mary's tiny face. "Use the glass under the mirror in the bathroom, Mary's glass"

"Calm down Mary Margaret, it's all right. Calm down. My God, she's hysterical! Separate those boys and stop yelling, Bud. I can't settle her down. She'll go into an asthma attack."

As Mary slowly sipped the water, she relaxed into her mom who rocked and sung to Mary. "That's it, relax. That's much better."

Mary looked up to see her father watching them. "How is my Mary Mar? It's OK, the boys were just fighting. That's what boys do."

Her father's smile did not reassure her. She closed her eyes and allowed her mother to rock her to sleep.

Mom goes to work

She sat backwards in the living room chair, with her arms
folded over the top and her head resting on them. The
curtain was pulled away from the window and placed in
back of her, separating her from the house and including
her with the outside world. Sniffling and wiping her
tears, she was determined to wait just like this until her
mom got home from work. She said a little prayer that
her brothers and sisters would leave her alone.

Mary was the oldest girl in the family, and the middle
child of seven. Ken, Shawn, Matt, Bill, Meghan and
Maeve surrounded her. She took care of the younger
children and sought the affection of her older brothers.
But lately it felt as if her place in the family was lost.

Since her mom started working a week ago, Mary was
miserable. Nothing made sense at home anymore. Her
brothers made up rules for her when it suited them. They
were always telling her to do their work, yelling at her.
Today, when she yelled back, her oldest brother slapped
her cheek. She could still feel the sting. She hoped that
she would be safe here, in her chair alone, waiting for
mom to come home and make sense of it all.

She knew her brother would be in trouble. In her family,
boys were not allowed to hit girls. She was glad about
this rule because her bothers fought and hurt each other
all the time, more now since mom started working. There
were lots of rules in her family about boys and girls. She
was not supposed to go many places that the boys could
go: the mall, the woods, town. She hated all those other
rules that excluded her. She liked this rule though
because it usually kept her from getting hit.

When she thought about it, she really did not want her brother to get into trouble. It would just mean more fighting in the house. She wanted the fighting to stop. It made her so unhappy.

Feeling a little cold from being so near the window, she wrapped the curtain around her like a blanket and prayed for her mother to drive her car up the driveway.

Control your emotions

As she gasped frantically for breath Mary's mother rubbed her back and spoke in soothing tones.

"Slow down, Mary Margaret. You need to learn how to control your emotions. It will be OK. Just slow down. Breathe slowly."

Mary's young mind reeled. How can you breathe slowly when you can't get enough breath to begin with? How can a person control their emotions? It didn't seem possible.

Thirst overwhelmed her as she struggled to get breath in through her open mouth. She could feel her chest heaving in and out with a vacuum like pressure.

Her sister brought some water and Mary slowly sipped it while her mother rubbed her hand in circles on Mary's small back. She closed her eyes and let the darkness soothe her. She pretended she was falling asleep and this calmed her body down. As breathing became easier, Mary nestled herself against her mother's warm body.

"That's it sweetheart, just slow down."

Sweat Room

Lifting herself out of a dream, she rolled over and pulled up the sheet. It brought a wave of coolness with it but that wouldn't last long. Throwing the sheet off and pulling it back up was her only activity on days that she spent in her bedroom with the door closed and the vaporizer on. Her only visitors were her mom and grandmother who brought food and drink or added water to the vaporizer.

Things had gotten easier at home since her grandmother came to live with her family. The boys did not fight so much. There was always someone to take care of Mary when she was sick.

Mary amused herself by watching drops of water race down the walls. They raced down the mirror faster, but she got tired of watching the mirror. When her asthma was out of control, her bedroom was converted to a steam room until her breathing improved. By then she usually had dropped several pounds and felt very weak. The long climb back to health was a familiar one.

Sometimes, she didn't even turn on the light when darkness fell. She watched the steam move through the moonlight. By the time someone came in with water to quench her thirst and a bite to eat, the light from the lamp hurt her eyes. She drifted in and out of sleep on days like this. Her only awareness of time came with the sun and the moon.

Her mom usually waited until Mary asked for the steamer in her room. She would wait to ask until she felt that if she fell asleep she wouldn't wake up. Until she felt that it hurt so much to breathe, she wasn't sure if she could take another breath. After that point, it was easy to lay in the steam room, it felt better.

The music on the radio sometimes invaded her dreams and the songs came alive with the characters and images that defined her. But sometimes, when she was calm enough and happy enough, she would turn out the lamp and compose music in her mind. As clouds of steam rose to meet the light of the moon, they created the images of the symphony in her mind that only she could hear and see. In that place between dreaming and awake, where heart and soul come alive, undisturbed by life outside the bedroom door, she flew.

Here she became comfortable with the sound of her own thoughts. She relied on imagination to pass the time. She was never really unhappy here, just sick. Never restless, simply waiting to get better. Always patient because it gave her time to amuse herself in her own world. A world where she was funny and smart. Where she listened to her own music and watched her own movies. Where she surrounded herself with herself and felt loved and understood. This world was the same dreaming and awake. That was the part she liked.

Comfortable fort

Leaves, branches, limbs, moss, trunk pieces were all she needed to build her home. The quiet, secluded, peaceful home where no one could bother her was built according to the specs of her imagination. She knew that she was probably too old to be building a fort in the woods. She also knew that eventually other kids would find it and wreck it, guided by some primal ritual that seemed unstoppable.

Since she was eight, shortly after her family had moved into the subdivision surrounded by a forest preserve, she had been coming to the woods for refuge from the disquieting world. Every day, if her dad was home when she left the house he would say, "stay out of the woods." And every day she headed right for them. The only trouble she ever found there was a wrecked fort.

New treasures were discovered every day. The river, so different at various spots in the woods was a source of adventure and calm, depending on her need. The river gave her whatever she needed without question, unconditionally. And there was the pond that would get quite large when it rained. Near the pond was a tree with a great vine strong enough for swinging on. Everyone would climb up the small embankment, hold the vine, and swing out into the pond, plop. They would come out muddy from the bottom and run to wait in line for another flight. Great fun.

Other times when she was feeling social there were the snow mobile-ers, the picnic-ers or the horseback riders. She got to know several people in the surrounding towns that rode their horses through the woods. Some lived less than an hour away on foot and she would visit them at home occasionally.

There were paths all over the woods. Most of them led to the nature center situated on a bank of the widest part of the river. There she could visit the owl, hawks, foxes, wolves all kept in a habitat at the center. Each building in the center had fascinating, interactive displays that rediscovered the mysteries of the woods, from bugs to ecosystems.

Down river from the center was a big clearing with a huge stone fire place in a shelter. When the weather got cold she would gather wood, start a fire and use a picnic table close to it as her reclining chair. She could sit and watch the fire for hours. After her friends discovered her, they began to look for her there on nice cold days, always sure to be able to warm themselves by her private fire. It was comforting that they would come and go while she tended the fire, dreaming the hours away. There were pumps for water all over the forest. The water was good, clear and cold and fresh tasting. No need to go home until the end of the day.

She raised herself in these woods when weather permitted. Deer came and went in peace as did bunnies, squirrels, fox, birds of all kinds. She had come to know many of the best trees, climbing them and staying perched for hours, watching and listening to the world go by. No family fights, no one to intrude, no expectations. She wanted to always remember these feelings, peace, freedom, comfort, joy. She did not see any adults having these feelings. And she vowed that as she grew, she would never loose them.

Use the Diary Mary Margaret

She woke up with the dream still going on in her mind. What a great dream. Not wanting to lose it, she rushed into the bathroom, where her mother was in front of the mirror getting ready for the day, to tell her all about it.

"Oh Mary Margaret, your dreams are so weird, I just can't listen to them. Use that diary that you got for Christmas and write them down if you need to tell someone about them. Honestly, they are so strange and crazy!"

A light went on in Mary's head. What a great idea! Write her dreams in the diary. She had not opened it since Christmas. A dream diary, what a brilliant idea!

"Thanks mom," she said breathlessly as she rushed to find the diary. Mary had not even heard her mother's opinions of her dreams. The criticism rolled off of her like water. The excitement of a new realm all her own was all her heart could hold. She could do this forever. It would be like a fort, made of dreams and words and soul. Finally, a fort that no one else could wreck!

Later, her mother found her still in her pajamas, writing furiously in the new dream diary. "Come on Mary Margaret, you have missed the bus. I will have to drive you to school. Honestly, if it isn't one thing it's another with you."

She was finished recounting her dream in the book anyway. Jumping up, she threw on some clothes and ran downstairs for breakfast without even combing her hair. She was much too happy about her world inside to let anything on the outside spoil it.

A room of her own

As she finished adjusting the mirror above her dresser, she admired her own smiling face. Finally, a room of her own. With three older brothers off to college, she was able to move into the smallest bedroom, a little cave where she could find peace.

This day was spent putting everything in her room in just the right place. The brass bells bought in Old Town were rearranged on the shelf several times around her candles. She loved burning candles and watching the flames as she meditated, although her father was always complaining that she would "burn the house down."

In her desk were her paints and pencils, sealing wax and colored papers. Everything needed for writing the most elaborate notes to her friends. In her closet, all the notes ever received were organized in shoe boxes and stacked neatly. Childhood treasures. On the back end of her closet floor was a blanket and a few tiny dolls that she secretly kept to play with, even though she was too old for dolls. This hidden fort provided her the setting for her most intimate conversations with the universe - no interruption, intrusion, or judgment.

She walked over to the stereo and put on a record. *A Song for the Asking* by Simon and Garfunkle helped create the mood. Propping pillows on her bed, she laid down and considered her new found peace and privacy. No matter what was going on outside that door, she was safe inside her room. Her own place. As she flattened her body out on the bed, she began the yoga relaxation exercises learned in gym class. Relax your toes. Relax your ankles. Relax your knees. Yours, and no one else's.

The fire from the candle light threw a glow over everyone's faces. She took a deep breath and let her short speech flow from her. She had practiced it so many times she did not even have to think about it now. "I light the fire of…"

She was ranked third in her 8th grade graduating class of 28 students. Her rank mandated that she be part of the candle lighting ceremony on graduation night. With so much uncertainty before her, it was hard to feel happy about leaving her school.

In eighth grade, there were two classes of fourteen students each. But some of the grades in the small school had been combined to have enough students. Her fourth and fifth grade classes were combined with the same wonderful teacher who had reinforced Mary's love of reading. She felt lucky to have this teacher for two years.

Stepping off the stage and back into the chorus, her class sang for the audience as the music teacher's daughter played piano and the music teacher herself played bells. They had practiced these songs for months and the harmonies proved it.

As the students sat down in their chairs, the principal prepared to read names and hand out diplomas. Mary looked at the picture of the school that hung on the gym wall and waited her turn. She would miss many teachers: her Science teacher, who gave extra lectures in Chemistry because Mary loved the subject; the English teacher, who taught her how to diagram sentences a paragraph long; the history teacher, who made her laugh about everything, including history. It was hard to leave, hard to let go.

She knew that here she was loved and respected. She did not know what would happen in high school.

As the ceremony ended, the sun was setting and the light in the gymnasium was changing by the second. She was the last to leave her chair, watching the scene, the light changing the people, the event. She felt frozen in time.

Grabbing Mary's hand, her friend pulled her out of the chair. "Come on Mayr, John wants to give you directions to the party."

Life went on.

Michael

As she lit the fire in the fireplace, she realized that this was the first "date" she had taken to this place that brought her so much happiness growing up. She stepped back as the sticks and paper caught fire and the flames roared up over the small logs. She went over to Michael who was trying to get comfortable on the picnic table after emptying the contents of Mary's bag of "supplies." He had looked at her with suspicion earlier, when she told him the bag was full of supplies that they would need on their date. She wanted to keep the destination a secret. She was sure he still did not know why she brought him to the woods at night or what was so terrific about this place. She would just have to get him to see the magic as the evening went on.

"Well, it looks like you remembered everything we will need for an evening in the woods!" he said. She could not tell whether or not he was being sarcastic.

"It doesn't look like much I know. But I wanted to do something a little different. We don't need to spend a lot of money or always be entertained. And we don't have to stay in where our families are there to be a part of our time together. In this place, I can share my growing up years, and I hope you can share yours with me. This place is full of memories and spots of quiet pleasure for me. The river, my favorite trees, the fire, even the water pumps have tender meaning for me. The water is delicious. Those are the things that were waiting for us here. I brought things to keep us comfortable. Blankets, snacks, drinks. You have been so easy to talk to and you must know, I have never shared this with a guy."

She could see him softening as she spoke. As she ended her explanation, a smile lit his face. He pulled her next to him on the picnic table and kept his arms around her. They both looked at the fire.

"I am proud to be your first."

She laughed at his insinuation. "Well," she said teasingly, "you could become many 'firsts' with me. For some, you will have to wait much longer than others."

She secretly hoped that her strict morals would be accepted with as much enthusiasm as her secret place in the woods. She liked Michael. He was the first boy to come along that she considered more than a date. He was a good student, a good athlete, a good listener. He liked to take her places that she had never been. She could tell he was proud to introduce her to people and happy whenever he saw her. And he was calling more and more.

She hoped he was considering of the possibility of a good, long term relationship. That is, as good as it can be at 15. Of course, he was 17. Two years older. But those particular two years meant a lot of maturity for an adolescent. His maturity made her comfortable. She liked that he knew where he was going to college and what he would study. She liked that he had gotten a full scholarship to be part of the wrestling team. He was not as uncertain about the future as most of the boys she knew. He seemed very self assured and determined to get close to her. She liked that too.

As they began to nibble on the snacks she brought, she noticed that the light was beginning to change from the sunset.

"Oh, before it gets dark, let me show you the river. It isn't far. I love the sound of it. Come on."

She grabbed his hand and they walked to the river bank with their arms around each other. As they sat by the river and watched the sunset through the trees, she told him about growing and playing in these woods. They talked about family and friends, hopes and dreams. She was glad he was the kind of boy who thought about those things and knew what he valued. They seemed to share a way of looking at the world and ambitions for the future.

Once the darkness of night finally descended, they walked back to the pavilion and put some more wood on the fire. Sharing a blanket, they sat back, put their feet up and resumed their talk.

Unexpectedly, Michael kissed her passionately and whispered "I love you." She did not know what to say. She sighed and hugged him hard. Just then she noticed the moon rising over the clearing. An enormous harvest moon of pure gold.

"Oh Mike, look at the moon. Come on, I will show you my favorite trees. I bet if we climb them, we will have a wonderful view of the moon."

"Mary, you are one fun date."

She spun to look at him, to see if he was making fun of her. But his eyes and smile showed her that he loved all of this as much as she did. And he loved her. Although she was not ready to tell him that she loved him too, she kissed him and then led him to the climbing tree.

I am sitting on my father's bed in his nursing home trying to comfort him, explain to him why he is here and who I am. I am really trying to remain with him, the father in my heart. His eyes are the deepest blue, a sea of terror. I must swim through these waters and breathe the light of peace that barely penetrates.

I dress myself in seaweed that strangles me and pulls me further into the depths, where I must loose control of myself and my emotions, or drown.

I am suddenly in my father's sterile room again. We are holding each other, rocking, crying. The order of the room is all around us. The world's order. Nature's order and purpose. And the only chaos is contained in the tears that stream down our faces.

Suddenly, I lose control of my body. I fly around the room and spin uncontrollably. I scream and cry and am lost outside of my body, yet vividly feel the motion and air as it flies like a wild, spastic bird trying to escape a cage. The soft blue warmth of my father's eyes brings me back to my body and back to calmness. We share the calm terror found in his eyes.

As I awaken from this dream my mind and spirit emerge as from a cocoon. Is this the mind's shelter of forgetfulness? Or an unconsciousness settling? The image in my mind as I wake is one of layers and layers of white lace, rising, being lifted from my eyes.

Trying them on for size

Studying herself in the mirror, she decided that tomorrow she would change her look again. This one was not much fun. Since Michael left for college, she had been dressing differently, more like the "hippies" at school. It was certainly comfortable, but set up expectations with people that she could not live up to. She enjoyed people asking her to cut class and go sing in the forest preserve. And she enjoyed this click's interest in world events and their idea that they were empowered to make change. But she did not like being expected to smoke pot with everyone or asked for drugs. And she needed to find a way to turn that around without losing her new friends.

Mary was discovering that the way she dressed effected the type of people that approached her for friendship. And she loved experimenting with this to meet different kinds of people and make new friends. Since Michael was gone and she was on her own, she enjoyed the freedom it gave her to be whoever she wanted to be. She was free to discover who she was without having to be what Michael expected. She could change herself without bothering anyone really. Her few close friends seemed to accept all of her changes without question.

But the hippie look had taken her into the 60's drug culture, a place she really did not want to be. She would often lie and say that she was already too high to avoid taking drugs passed to her.

Looking for a way out, she changed her clothes to some much more preppie. Kilts, sweaters, Capezio shoes. She liked this too because she actually enjoyed wearing skirts. But many of the hippie friends that she made would not associate with her now. With Michael gone, she did not seem to fit in anywhere. The problem might be, she wanted to fit in everywhere but was forced to choose a group by some unspoken rule of adolescence.

She had two years before she could join him at college. It would be a long two years if she kept drifting from one group to another. Each group had their good and bad qualities. It was fun to hear everyone's stories and see how each fit into the group. But now she had to find a way to keep friends from each group as she moved around the school. She wondered if anyone else had this problem. Everyone seemed content to stay in their own niche.

She headed to the school library to do a little fashion research. Thumbing through a magazine, she stopped at a picture of a model in draw string pants and an oversized top. She wondered if that look would help her in her next change. She studied the picture a long time before moving on to look for more inspiration. It was a good thing her mom worked for a women's clothing company.

After school, she slid into the car next to her mother. "Hi mom, could I shop for clothes tonight?"

"What is next Mary Margaret? I was glad to see you get rid of that old clothes look."

"Nothing that bad, just a little different. The kids are calling me a "Rah rah." I am not sure what that is, but I need to change."

"I sure will be glad when Michael comes home. You are much more predictable when he is around."

"And you think that's a good thing? Can we stop for a coke, I am really thirsty."

"Anything else Rah ra?"

"Please, that's not even funny. I miss Mike too"

I am standing on a bridge that goes over a huge river. I am waiting for a boat to come and take me on a ride.

I reach into the pocket of my coat and find a jar of bubbles. While I wait I blow bubble after bubble, until I am surrounded by shiny bubbles of all different sizes. This delights me. The bubbles don't pop or go too far from me. The more bubbles I create, the more I am surrounded by them. I admire the rainbows within them. I consider their individuality in shape and size.

A flock of white birds flies over and carries the bubbles off to distant places. This makes me very happy, as if it was meant to be.

Roaring with laughter, her body bumped into Viv's as she came to a stop at the bottom of the small hill. They both continued to giggle until their heads stopped spinning and their bodies stopped aching. Rolling down the hill had become a good way to let go of the tensions of adolescence.

She and Viv had stumbled on this great spot as they were wandering around Vivian's neighborhood, talking, the way teenagers do. Viv became her closest friend in high school during freshman year. Having come from a small, satellite school in the district, Mary was a little overwhelmed by the high school of 2000 students. She kept mostly to herself, listening closely to everything around her. Vivian had chosen to befriend her. They shared English class. By the end of the year Vivian was seated next to her so that they could pass notes easily. She told Mary that she liked her answers in class and thought she had a great laugh.

Vivian represented stability in the larger world of high school to Mary. She had come from the large, core Junior High School and seemed to be friends with everyone. But her best friend was an exotic girl named Katrina who Mary loved to watch. She was so self assured, very outspoken, not cut from any mold.

When Katrina moved away, Viv turned more and more to Mary. She loved to spend time at Mary's house with all the chaos and activity that seven children bring. She dated Mary's brother Matt on and off so that on some weekends, Mary felt that she was competing with her brother for Viv's company. But sometimes, all three just went out together. Viv really liked Michael, and they double dated when he was home from school.

During their junior year in high school, they spent more evenings in their secret place that they called the "Coliseum." It was actually the back yard of a local publishing company whose property was near Vivian's neighborhood. The grass dipped down creating a small hill leading to a lower level glass wall. The night lighting from the empty building shed a romantic hue. The rest of the property above was beautifully landscaped with large trees and flower gardens. When the girls stood down by the glass of the building, they felt surrounded by the hill and imagined they were surrounded by an audience.

The girls liked to come down here after dark and dazzle each other with recitations from Shakespeare. Sometimes, they both took a part, watching their own performance mirrored in the glass. For soliloquies or sonnets, one would sit on the hill and become the audience, stirring up crowd noises like a fire, driving the drama further along. They often brought bottles of water with them so that thirst could not drive them home.

Sometimes, they would roll their bodies down the hill for the fun of it. Laying flat on their tummies at the top, all they had to do was turn over and their bodies rolled over and over, faster and faster until they stopped just short of the building at the bottom. There, the girls stayed until their vision cleared, or they stopped crying from the laughter.

Often, they lay on their backs on the hill and watched the stars through the trees. It was the perfect spot to take a stab at understanding the universe and their place in it. What were they here for? Why do people do the things they do? What place do they want for themselves? Where will they be in 40 years? What really matters, and what doesn't? What makes life worth living? What's it all about? The stars, and the love of their friendship led the way.

The gift of Barbie

The wind blew hard and cold into the house as Ken
opened the door. He and his family rushed inside to
escape the bitter winter weather. "Merry Christmas one
and all," he roared with a laugh.

Michael had not yet arrived to join in the family
Christmas Eve celebration. Mary sat silently as the new
arrivals were greeted. She was worried about him driving
so far in this bad weather. But she was excited about her
gift to Ken's daughter Crissy. She decided to give her
Barbie trunk full of clothes and accessories. The original
Barbie doll with the curl still in her blonde ponytail was
also part of the package. Mary did not really play with
these toys much, but her mother insisted on buying them
thinking that every girl should have a doll collection.
Mary never felt the excitement of putting the clothes on
and off a doll. She much preferred her places and friends
in the woods or a good book.

Most of the clothes were in perfect condition because
they went from the package to the trunk and were not
touched again. The barbecue outfit had all of the little
utensils in the apron pocket. The wedding dress and veil
had never been worn.

When Michael arrived she relaxed and joined in the
festivities. He got along well with her family, including
her three older brothers who were known for scaring her
dates off. Even her grandmother loved him and treated
him like a special guest in the house. All of the flowers
and gifts he had sent to the house over the past two years
impressed Grandmother more than Mary.

Mary simply loved the way he made her feel when she
was with him, complete, loved, wonderful, excited. She

trusted him completely and had revealed everything about her before finally telling him she loved him. He waited patiently for that, never once complaining that he was saying it long before she was. She finally whispered it one night over dinner at the Como Inn, downtown Chicago while Lou Rawls played piano and crooned. And now she whispered it to him as she welcomed him in from the cold with a hug.

Everyone gathered around the Christmas tree to open presents. It was a big crowd that spanned four generations and included boyfriends, girlfriends and a couple of plain old friends. Their Christmas was much enjoyed by all and the sparse, outdated decorations were gladly overlooked. Her family did not put much money into Christmas, but always managed to have a good time. That is, if Dad could stay sober and Grandmother calm.

Her mother put some Christmas music on the stereo. Bells chimed sweetly in the background of a *White Christmas* instrumental. Then she turned down the lights to relax everyone. The babies were overly excited in anticipation. Grandma was overly excited because of all the people in the house.

She sat back on the couch with Michael's arm around her. After looking up at him and drinking in his face, she closed her eyes and let her head swim with the smell of him. Suddenly, she heard a small gasp and then silence. When she opened her eyes she saw Crissy looking through the Barbie trunk and her mom moving down on the floor to help. Everyone turned and looked at Mary in amazement. She did not know why this gift was so surprising.

"Well that will be worth a lot of money some day. There is Crissy's college fund," her brother Ken laughed. Suddenly she understood everyone's amazement. They were thinking about how much money the collection was worth. She had not even considered it when she chose this gift for her niece.

"Are you sure about this?" Crissy's mom asked.

"Well, I imagined her playing with it, not selling it. But whatever Crissy decides, it is hers now. All the little accessories are in the trunk drawers."

"Mary took very good care of that collection," her mother chimed in proudly.

Another surprise to Mary. She really had not liked the collection and did not play with it. She appreciated her mother's pride anyway.

As Michael drew her closely to him she whispered "time to give up my childhood."

He had asked her to marry him while he was home on Thanksgiving break. She said yes, but asked him to keep the engagement unofficial until she could join him at school next fall. She was not sure why, she just felt that was the way it should be. They quietly watched the rest of the festivities while they cuddled.

Billy's Belt

As she walked up the driveway she turned her face to the sunlight to enjoy its warmth. Her mind replayed the best parts of the day.

Her creative writing class had chosen her poem on Viet Nam as the best of the class. Because of that, two wonderful people approached her. She made two new friends that day.

Thomas sought her out in the cafeteria and poured his heart out. She could still feel the touch of his hand and the smell of his shoulder as she embraced him. His friendship always made her smile.

Michael would call tonight. She missed him terribly. She was beginning to feel the pain of having the man she loved at college while she finished high school. She was her best when she was with him. He always made her feel that way.

Before she opened the door she could hear her father yelling. She hesitated, trying to hear the words and get a picture of what was going on inside the house. Impulse pushed her ahead into the house. She saw her father flying up the stairs with his belt in his hand, cursing and yelling. She kicked off her shoes, dropped her books and purse on the desk and in seconds was in her younger brother's room.

"Dad, stop. Daddy, stop," she heard herself yelling. Moving against her fear she reached over and pulled her father away from her brother before he could issue the next blow.

Her father's wild eyes met hers. The moment froze and she could hear nothing. All that existed were those eyes that she met full on.

"Dad, stop hurting him," she said in a low firm tone. Her father's eyes closed and he left the room quickly and quietly.

She turned her attention to her brother, who lay on his bed curled in a ball, sobbing. As she reached out to him, he cried, "don't touch me."

"Billy, let me help you."

"Just leave me alone" he yelled and curled tighter into his protective ball.

"OK Bill." She slowly left the room and closed the door. She could hear him crying as she turned to leave. She shook her head to try to get rid of the realization that no one in the family would ever mention this event afterward. No one would come up to help Billy through his pain. He was too young to have so much pain. Without a second thought she walked out of the house. She saw no one and nothing; all a dark blur. Her heart pounded wildly and her body was numb.

It wasn't until she was in the woods, half way to the clearing that she was able to think with any clarity. She was out of breath, but did not know if that was from running, or hyperventilating. She could not remember a thing from the time she left Bill's room until now. Where was she going?

She decided to climb her favorite tree and give herself a chance to calm down. As she reached the clearing, a warm breeze touched her face and she turned to greet it with a smile. She pushed a picnic table over to the tree and climbed half way up. Nestling herself into the cradle of the tree she embraced it, and thanked it.

She wrapped the clearing around her like a thick comforter. The trees, the shelter, the water pumps, the wood fence that ran along the bridal path all provided certainty and stability. She kept all thought from her mind and focused instead on the comfort of her favorite place. Once her heartbeat quieted enough, she could hear the river running in the distance. She slowly fell asleep as her mind and body calmed.

Goodbye Michael

"Mary, Granny wants to know if you are going to eat dinner."

'No," she said into her pillow. She heard the door shut but did not look up.

She knew she was loosing weight lately, but could not bring herself to eat.

She heard the door open again. "Mary, Michael is on the phone. Will you talk to him?" her grandmother asked.

"No," she whispered without looking up. Her Grandmother said nothing and shut the door.

Mary wished that Michael would just stop calling. She really had nothing more to say to him. And she had no intention of forgiving him and resuming the relationship. He had been calling nearly everyday for over a month. At first she took the calls and told him the same things again and again. Finally, she just stopped taking the calls. They were always the same. He felt miserable and wanted her back. He felt miserable. Good. Why should she be the only one to feel that way after what he had done?

Mary took the train to visit Michael about a month ago. The idea was spontaneous. She had been telling a friend that day in school that she missed him. He offered to drive her to the train station. She packed her bag and left after school. She had such high hopes as she got out of his car and said goodbye to board her train.

At the time, she thought nothing of her surprise visit. She visited Michael two or three times a year since he went to college. But when she called him from the train station, he seemed anxious. Not at all the reception she expected.

When he came to pick her up he was nervous. But he could not say that anything specific was wrong. When they got back to his room he seemed to relax. But when they started kissing she knew that something was different. It was as if she was kissing a stranger. When she asked him if he had been kissing someone else, confession poured out of him like flood water over a river bank. Her life had not been the same since.

After the initial anger and shock from his confession, she felt only numb and depressed. She spent her days thinking about all the signals and signs that she just didn't see. She felt blind and stupid.

It turned out that Michael had been seeing someone else at college. The same someone else for well over a year. Mary had been introduced to this someone else his Freshman year. Miss Someone Else was part of the crowd Michael hung around with at school. Mary had often talked to her during her visits to Michael and confided some of the history of her relationship with Michael. Mary now knew had been played by Miss Someone Else. And betrayed by Michael.

The fact was that Mary and Michael had agreed to wait until they were married to have sex. She knew this was a romantic notion, but was happy when Michael agreed. It had saved her a moral dilemma. But Michael readily admitted that he and Miss Someone Else had no such arrangement. They had shared the intimacy that Mary and Michael were saving until marriage. This was the ultimate insult.

Mary revealed herself completely to Michael. She believed in him with her whole heart. She knew that love, for her, would never again have this implicit trust or devotion.

She was left wondering what Michael actually got out of his relationship with her. Why had he stayed with her? What did he expect of her? And then Mary stopped wondering. She stopped caring what he was thinking or what he felt. She felt only cold when she thought of him.

As time went on she could not lift herself out of this pit of sadness. All of her screams were silent. She did not have the energy for anger. She rarely said a word to anyone and spent most of her time in her room, sleeping. She did not even go to the woods for comfort. She had little interest in people or activities and less patience for the problems in her family. She had no idea how to pull herself out of it and no energy to try. Her family just left her alone. No one even asked why.

She vaguely decided not to go to college next year. Her 18th birthday was in a couple of weeks. She would be free to move out of her parents house and get away from that chaos. It would leave some time before graduation. She knew that she should at least finish high school. If she handed in her last few papers, she could probably skate through. Everyone stopped paying attention to her attendance and grades a long time ago. The school did not even complain in the atmosphere of "open campus."

She had some older friends who were encouraging her to move in with them. Their rental homes were considered "communes," but Mary was beyond caring what anyone thought. She felt a desperate need to escape. She began spending the weekends there already. They built bonfires in the back yard at night, and she liked to sit and listen to the conversations. She rarely contributed. When she got tired she would go into the house and fall asleep on the couch. She didn't bother changing her clothes all weekend. It never occurred to her to care enough to do that simple task.

She had saved a little money for college since she started working at age 14. It would give her some time to get away and work things out. She knew she was in bad shape and needed to do something to change things. This was all she could think of. At least it was something.

I am sitting in my room next to a candle that flickers light into the darkness. A cat, with glowing green eyes is jumping around, chasing flying bugs that are not there. I get up and open my door. I see a long corridor that is not familiar. I look down to see that I am barefoot and worry that I will hurt my feet if I leave my room.

Instead, I close the door and pick up a guitar. Most of the strings are broken but I still manage to play a slow, sad tune. A sudden wind in the room blows out the candle and I am left in darkness.

Light on the hill

The grass at the top of the hill was moist and fragrant. It tickled her nose as she breathed in and out. The music of Van Morrison surrounded her coming from speakers on the east and west sides of the hill. The owner's of the farm had gone to great lengths to include music into their piece of heaven here in Black Earth, Wisconsin. Rolling hills, corn fields, quiet, isolation, everything she needed to sort things out for herself. Laying motionless, she let herself drift into the hill and away with the music, her emotions running together the like distant bells in the music's counterpoint.

Here she was, taking time off between high school and college to decide what she wanted. Time to search her heart. Time away from everyone. She was glad to be asked to look after this place while the owners spent the summer elsewhere. But she had no idea where to go from here. Michael was gone. She missed a partner. She still was not used to being alone. But it certainly opened up the possibilities of the future for her. No one else's plans to include. No where to go particularly. What did she want out of life? What did she have to offer? What would bring her joy? Where could she succeed? She felt like an eighteen year old question mark.

She closed her eyes and fell into the darkness. As her body calmed and breathing slowed, the darkness became the light. This was the place that she had learned to go inside to find answers, a place of no direction and no bounds. This was a place of peace and joy and whatever she brought to it. Here she brought the question mark that weighed heavily across her shoulders. Here she could lay it to rest and drift away.

When Mary woke the sun was setting over the hills and corn. She had a moment when she was not placed in time and did not recognize the space. She reluctantly let go of the peace and light that pervaded her rest. Sitting up, she looked around and breathed deeply the sweet moist air of twilight. The world was perfectly quiet but for the birds. She was tempted to lay back down and sort out their songs before orchestrating them into one harmony again. But she resisted. There was a question and answer to remember. What was it?

Slowly she became aware of the certainty that rest had given her. She did need to go to college. She needed to write above all. Which college? Should she teach? Include other studies? Those questions could wait for another day. But she was certain that she needed to get to college and study writing. It would not be easy to get there. She alienated her parents when she moved out before finishing high school. They were probably still angry that she did not attend her graduation ceremony. Michael's betrayal made life at home intolerable. She felt she had been drowning in her family's problems with no room to breathe and sort out her own. She had no money to speak of and few possessions. It would take effort to find her way back into the good graces of her family. It was the only way to make college possible.

Walking down the hill she sighed with wonder. She had plenty of time to think it all through before returning home to repair the damage.

I had so much fun this weekend up in "Rip-on." Our first year in college has been great. I suppose I will be spoiled when I finally get to Southern and really have to study. It has been wonderful coming to see you on the (almost every) weekend.

Yes, I have decided to join Matt at Southern. So much time for such a simple decision. In the end, I really wanted to spend some more time with him AND go to college. We share some friends down there from the home town....I needed the connection.

Will you order me a copy of the Ripon yearbook? Too bad my picture is in it more than you or any of your friends. Ha Ha. Some kind of poetry there. I especially like the picture of us by the lake. The light on the water makes it all so dreamy. We look happy to be together.

It has been wonderful to come up and see you so often this year while I took my hiatus from school. I am glad I took a year off to decide what I actually wanted to study. And I guess I am glad that you will be going to a school better suited for you next year. But you will be so far away in Berkley. I will have to come visit spring breaks for sure. We sure had fun our freshman year at Ripon didn't we?

Well, we each, in our own way, took the year to find direction. Now we are off. Please stay in touch. I love you.

mmb

Special Major

"You are not the first student to tell me their troubles with the Creative Writing department. I have the advantage of insider knowledge because I come from the English Department. The Creative Writing instructors think that their methods are the best way to teach students to become productive writers. By productive, I mean writers that can get paid for writing when they leave college. I can't say as I agree, but it is not my decision."

The Dean of Liberal Arts continued, "I have been doing a little research on you. You are known in the department for being very bright and hard working. But you are also known to be ground breaking, experimental. It is not a wonder that you do not fit into their models and methods. But I think I can help."

"We have just started a program in the College of Liberal Arts called 'Special Major.' It basically allows students to write their own majors using hours in any department within the College of Liberal Arts. You will be the second student enrolled in this program. Take the catalog home and consider how to create a major centered around your writing. Along with the departmental classes, there is independent study in each department and 20 hours of independent study offered through the LA college."

"That means many of your credit hours can be independent study, but you will need to produce something. Your studies will become project driven. Do you understand what I mean?"

"Yes!" Mary lit up. "My writing is based on visual imagery because I think it has the most profound effect on the reader. Maybe I could come up with something centered on that idea."

She was becoming quite excited now. Funny, when she came into the room, she thought she had hit a brick wall with the University. Suddenly, the wall became a door.

"I want you to think about staging some of your writing. Have you ever been interested in writing plays?"

"Well, it is certainly something I will consider."

"Good. A stage production would provide the project and the product for us to grade. I can sponsor your independent study within the college, but you will need to convince a departmental teacher to sponsor your studies within their department. I know most of the departmental heads. We can set up appointments for you to meet with them once you have put your Special Major proposal together."

"Bring it to me as soon as you have it and we'll go over it. Leave yourself enough time to make changes. You will need to finish the classes you are enrolled in this semester, so you will have plenty of time before winter semester registration."

"Now, I have to run. I am late for a meeting."

"Thank you so much sir. I can't thank you enough."

"Well, bring me your proposal, and we will see where we can take this."

Mary stood, shook hands with the Dean, and raced out of the building to get air. A cool wind hit her face and she closed her eyes to savor it.

She walked to the small lake in the quad and sat beneath her favorite tree. Closing her eyes, she tried to relax and process what just happened. This was one of those moments that causes a complete change in direction. She needed to take an inventory of all she had and where it might take her. There were so many stories in Mary waiting to be written. They rang within her like a symphony of bells.

Mary began to meditate to quiet herself. To quiet her emotion so that she could think clearly. It took awhile to reach that place without thought. She could not let go of the smile on her face.

I am in an unfamiliar shop. A small store with many glass display cases all filled with buttons. Buttons of all kinds filled the shelves, all very beautiful.

A young man with long hair tied back stood behind the case and gave me every button I asked to examine. I did not want to give any back because they were so beautiful. But I knew that I had to choose one. One button was all I needed. I don't know why only one or what it was needed for. But I knew I had to choose one out of all of them,

There were buttons made of pearl, emerald, turquoise, diamond, lapis. Some were made of common materials like clay but crafted exquisitely into shapes of insects, faces, hands, all different shapes.

Finally I chose a large button made of Lapis Lazuli after admiring the deep blue color and the thick gold veins running through it. The button had two small holes in the center and I thought I could use it for a sweater.

After paying the man, I turned to leave the store and a blue and yellow butterfly landed on my hand. I stepped out of the store and closed my eyes while the cool breeze on my face made me smile.

I got the bad news from home today that my dad has been diagnosed with Alzheimer's. His company has retired him early with benefits (thankfully.) My family has not really been keeping me informed about his deterioration. I have not been home since last Christmas. Then all I noticed was that he was unusually quiet.

I have known for a long time that he was changing, but truthfully, I thought it was his drinking.

Anyway, my mom is looking at nursing homes now. Apparently, there is a waiting list for the good ones in the area. In the mean time, my brother Bill is leaving college to take care of him. Ironic, that Bill is the one to take care of him. I think he had the least loving relationship with my father. There is a real puzzle.

I am sorry that I can't be there for my family, but glad to be away from the sadness. And guilty for the gladness. I can admit that to you. Thanks.

Let me know how you are doing.

Love,

mmb

Through the trees

Laying on her back, she propped her feet up on the tree and moved her bottom as close as she could to the base of the trunk. The view up into the tree was gorgeous. Autumn was peaking. Color surrounded her and soothed her.

As she shot a succession of pictures, she became vaguely aware of someone standing near her. When she finished, she looked up and saw another student taking her picture!

After laughing because she was caught in an awkward position, she explained to the school paper reporter that she was taking pictures to use as slides in the play she was producing. By the end of the semester, she was scheduled to stage a play that she spent the summer writing.

She had not named the play yet. It was complicated, poetic and somewhat obscure (or so she'd been told.) The play did not really need to be named until the PR was printed. She thought about it every day.

Today, she explained to the reporter that as part of her Special Major in "Visual Efficacy," she would put on this play on a small stage in the speech department, chosen for it's intimate, interactive feel for the audience. It was a multi media production that included set design, live music, actors, dancers, slides and paintings of images from the play.

Mary tried to give as much information as she could without being too specific. The truth was, she had not figured out all the specifics. This was her third small production at school, but the biggest one yet. A million decisions yet to be made.

The reporter thanked her and Mary turned to walk to class. The chapel's bells began to ring and she knew that she was late. But while she was walking, she noticed a huge burning bush next to the Humanities building that had an incredible ray of sunlight flowing through it. The light created a spectrum of red and orange color in the bush that only a picture could describe. Another picture or two, class could wait.

The happening

Berkley was a place to flourish. There was nothing she liked better than to visit Viv during her college breaks. Her school did not have the same semester schedule, thankfully. Mary flew out as often as she could to spend time sharing Viv's world.

Viv attended an Art school in Berkley. Mary would shadow her from class to class, participating when she could or helping Viv with her projects. Mary had been commended by the teacher in the life drawing class. She was shocked. It was the first time she tried to draw a nude model. She didn't know she had it in her. In high school, she took as many Science and English courses as she could, never an Art course.

Berkley was amazing. Viv was sharing a house with friends on the same block that Patti Hearst was kidnapped. Rows of old provincial homes that had become student housing. Kurt Vonnegut's daughter was in the class they were now walking into. In Contemporary Art class the students were presenting their projects. The assignment was simply "blood." Mary had donated some of hers to Vivian's project the night before by pricking her fingertips and smearing her blood wherever Viv wanted her to. Viv loved this class because the presentations were often wild and exciting.

Lisa, one of Viv's roomates, was presenting today. She asked everyone to step out into the parking lot. The small group gathered around her car as she put on boots, a long rain coat, rubber gloves and a rain hat. She then opened her trunk and pulled out two cases of open tomato juice cans. After closing the trunk, she poured the juice into a bucket and threw it all over her car. When she was finished, she got into her car and turned on the radio to blast some song about blood that Mary didn't recognize. Then she drove the car back and forth, moving in different directions in the parking lot. When the car finally stopped, she got out and took a bow during the classes' applause. Mary wished she had as much freedom in her studies. Her projects all required intensive work. Her state school would never accept such whimsy.

After class, Mary and Viv walked hand in hand up a hill to a spectacular view of the sunset over the ocean. They giggled and reminisced as color painted the sky like a painting in motion. After the sun was gone and there was barely any light left in the sky, they returned to Vivian's house to make dinner.

Lisa was busy in the living room working on her next project, a sculpture of mirrors. As they entered the kitchen, Viv suddenly turned and gave Mary a hug.

"I feel so much more like myself when you are here. I wish you could just stay."

"How can you miss me if I don't go away?" Mary asked with a laugh.

I am sitting on my father's bed in his nursing home trying to comfort him, explain to him why he is here and who I am. I am really trying to remain with him, the father in my heart. His eyes are the deepest blue, a sea of terror. I must swim through these waters and breathe the light of peace that barely penetrates.

I dress myself in seaweed that strangles me and pulls me further into the depths, where I must loose control of myself and my emotions, or drown.

I am suddenly in my father's sterile room again. We are holding each other, rocking, crying. The order of the room is all around us. The world's order. Nature's order and purpose. And the only chaos is contained in the tears that stream down our faces.

Suddenly, I lose control of my body. I fly around the room and spin uncontrollably. I scream and cry and am lost outside of my body, yet vividly feel the motion and air as it flies like a wild, spastic bird trying to escape a cage. The soft blue warmth of my father's eyes brings me back to my body and back to calmness. We share the calm terror found in his eyes.

As I awaken from this dream my mind and spirit emerge as from a cocoon. Is this the mind's shelter of forgetfulness? Or an unconsciousness settling? The image in my mind as I wake is one of layers and layers of white lace, rising, being lifted from my eyes.

Vivian,

Soul to soul…

I've tried to collect and organize my thoughts on our journals. Let me articulate some of my reactions…

It seems to me that over the years, the course of our thoughts and ideas run parallel. This explains why the two of us remain so mysteriously an inspiration to one another. We are making many of the same discoveries apart. Our spirits are one in the same through many depths. And this is why your spirit is so much a part of me. And why I need you so for my own expression. I cannot imagine this world without an usness between our two spirits: the dreams, the images, the wants, the needs, the drives, the isolation, all expressions of the spirit. In these, we are very much one, to this day. Amazing and marvelous.

It seems to me that we both have long, sometimes tedious cycles of inspiration. We need to dwell within and explore the depths of inactivity and despair before we can rediscover inspiration, elation, strength toward the world…but more importantly, toward our work. I do not think this process uncommon to creativity, but I think the length of the cycles and the depths of our extremes is somewhat uncommon. Many artists need to remain in one or the other extreme before they can express or create. Many artists bind themselves to a particular area within these extremes and so eventually limit and stifle themselves for the sake of contemporary style or political overtone. However, it seems to me that creativity itself is unlimited and cannot be organized too readily. That style and coherence is dependent on images of the spirit through which, creativity is ignited and is born. The spirit is always in flux as is reality. And only through the exploration of greater depths and extremes can one develop creatively. You seem to express this through your entries. In this we are one.

We also seem to share an intrinsic basis in dream and insanity or the unconscious (ungoverned sanity?) We have always shared our dreams. In my dreams, when I go insane, it is a flight. My head opens and my body loses control. Thoughts, images, colors, sounds, tastes, feelings all swirl and I lose everything I have ever known. Sometimes this evokes fear. In dream, I do not feel a responsibility toward reality. I am less earth bound so that the insanity becomes much more of a relief than a terrifying burden.

Dream then becomes "the screaming lull of quiet," or my silent scream. Although I may not come out of this dream with any coherent thoughts or feelings, more often than not, my inspirations come more steadily. The insanity of dream may therefore become a relief to the insanity of reality. It may push inspiration toward the surface. The spirit pushing through where the mind is too confused or stressed to make way for it. Where "the mind is riddled with too many thoughts." Are we one in this too? It sounds like it.

We are also alike in our search for any semblance to our own metaphysic. I am able to express my own metaphysic to you better than anyone else. I can identify these thoughts and ideas to you better than anyone.

You reference Descartes in your journal. I cannot agree with much of his thinking because he believes thought to originate with the intellect. In this I tend to lean more toward Croce and others that believe thought to originate with the spirit. That essence remains outside the intellect, in no-thing-ness. That inspiration comes only when we can step outside intellectual constraints. That my values

are what constitute my reality and these essences
constitute my values.

In a very strange way, we are alike in our ideas of space -
time - color - light - darkness. This must be evident to
you in reading my latest play. I say this is strange because
we work in different mediums. Perhaps this is where my
surrealistic roots come in, with my emphasis of elemental
images used to evoke a question of consciousness. I do
not write about nature but within it. To express me is to
express a purity, a space - time - eternity and essence, a
complete glimpse through me. Yet when expression is
complete, it is unchangeable. I am changed, however,
and must begin again to seek a different expression with
all of me. This is the only sense of measure in my art.

Let me know if I have hit the spot with any of this. And
let me know what you think.

mmb

Without a Word

It had been three days since her play "Without a Word" had been staged in a Chicago theater. Now, as she sat in Peg's apartment making follow up phone calls, she wondered at the emptiness she felt inside.

She sat looking at the phone. Her hand was still on the receiver in the cradle. She didn't want to let go. She didn't want the last call to end, but didn't know what to say to continue it.

Sitting back in her chair, she took in a big long breath and let it out slowly to try to gain her bearings.

"Sitting here, just sitting here damn it. Not even sitting here now. Just sitting."

The opening line in her play was coming back to haunt her. She was just as paralyzed as the character in her play, unable to move, think, get on with life. Funny, she thought, when she originally wrote that play, it released her from paralysis. The first time she staged it, it took her months to process everything that she had learned from it. It wasn't until she took the time to relax and reflect afterward that she was able to take what she had learned from the experience and move on. A valuable lesson.

But now, after the second staging in a theater in Chicago, she found herself overwhelmed and unable to process all that had happened. Her play had been successful on many levels. But all she could see was the failure of it. All she could feel was depression.

Removing her hand from the telephone, she remembered the call that whisked her into this reverie. The head of the drama department at Columbia College in Chicago asked her to stage the play again on their campus. Yesterday, someone from Lake Forest College had called asking the same. Why couldn't she see this as a huge success?

The little production company that she threw together from the remaining enthusiasm of the last production of her play was named "Agony and Ecstasy Productions." Mary was billed as the writer/director. Her friend Peggy, her "producer/designer" had been the pivotal character "mirror" in the original production. Mirror's scream from time to time had been central to the play. The character's scream was transformed throughout the play from half hearted to ear shattering, silent to heard.

Mary could feel herself silently screaming now. She did not understand what prevented her from screaming out loud. She felt she did not have the energy. Closer to the truth would be that she did not have the insight. Her pain prevented her from seeing or screaming. She did not see the resemblance to her own character.

The new production company consisted of people who had volunteered to be a part of the first production, as well as people who had seen the play and loved it so much, they wanted to be a part of the next staging. All were volunteers. Some had no idea when volunteering how much time and commitment a successful production would take.

The press described the play as "A new dimension in Art," "psychotheraeutics," and "a voyage into self discovery." The music was live, performed by a local band who played Argent's "Hold Your Head Up," along with other original jazz pieces. The band originally fought playing anything but original score, but Mary had persuaded them. Their version of the song lifted her heart to where it needed to be during the rehearsals.

But Mary discovered that she lacked the ability as a director to keep the crew on task. She did not have the assertiveness needed to convince volunteers to give their best effort. She did not have the ability to articulate ideas and feelings well enough for effective rehearsals. But most of all she did not understand that all of this came with experience in directing. Something only time could give her. Something for which she did not, by nature, have the requisite skills.

Mary grew up the peacemaker. Her solutions were always the fastest means toward peace. A good director needs to dig in, indulge the conflict with courage, and make sure that the players all develop the vision of their characters. That all players were where they needed to be and speaking their vision of the characters. There was too much in Mary's world that she was unwilling to face, to ever indulge herself in this process, let alone lead a group through it.

Then there was the thought of her father. The memory of him sent her immediately spiraling into depression. Her brother Shawn and his wife Pat brought him to opening night as a surprise to her. Her father had been confused and disoriented. He could not walk without assistance. Some of the avant-garde content of the multi-media production had disturbed him and he created somewhat of a scene in the audience.

She had not realized that her father's condition had degenerated so far. She wondered how much longer he would hold on. All of her unresolved feelings for her father now weighed heavily on her. This just added a new dimension to the feelings of failure attached to the production of her play.

She felt overwhelmed at the thought of all the energy it would take to pull together another crew and produce the play again at a different location. She was not sure if she had it, and unsure about where to get it. The self awareness and reflection needed to begin again was too painful right now.

The tremendous stress created by producing the play in Chicago had created a great deal of friction on some of her most important friendships. It had put a strain on her school schedule and she took "incomplete" in a couple of classes to focus on the play. And now she was pulled into her family's experience of struggling with the slow, painful death of an Alzheimer's victim.

She reached over and turned on a lamp. She had not noticed the light leaving the room and wondered how long she had been sitting in the dark.

Deciding that the only thing to do was postpone any decisions until she was feeling better, she stood, gathering her strength to pack and return to school. A great deal of hard work was waiting for her. She was reaching the end of her senior year. No decision about her future had yet been made. Moving to California to be near Viv sounded nice. Continuing school sounded nice. Staging the play as many times as possible might lead to opportunities.

With a heavy sigh, she pushed all of these thoughts out of her mind for a better day. Right now, the trip back to school was all she could handle.

Goodbye Dad

Driving slowly to make sure her Grandmother was comfortable, she shifted nervously in the driver's seat. She willingly volunteered to drive her Grandmother home early from her father's wake. It was just too much excitement for Granny, and Mary was glad for the break.

Never having gotten along well with Granny, Mary was comfortable with the silence on the way home. Since the day her Grandmother moved into the family home, there was a rivalry between them that Mary did not understand until years later. Granny was always very hard on Mary and her mother was always intervening. It was her Grandmother that felt compelled to break the silence.

"Bob seems like a nice boy Mary. Let's see, you have probably been dating him longer than anyone since Michael."

Her Grandmother had never forgiven her for that break up. But then again, Mary had not shared the details.

"Yes, I guess that is true. I didn't date anyone for long after Michael. Bob doesn't have a lot of needs. He is willing to work around my hectic class schedule and be there whenever I have the time, which is not often. Guys usually lose interest because of my limited availability. I just want to get through school as quickly as possible."

Granny made a noise, indicating that she heard and understood, but Mary doubted that. The rest of the ride home was silent, while Mary remembered how Bob held her when she cried after visiting her father in the nursing home. He just held her. Did not say anything. It seemed to be just what she needed. He was always there when she needed him.

Mary helped her Grandmother out of the car and into the house because it was dark and cold. Heading back to the Funeral Home she turned on the radio and sang along to Laura Brannigan's *Bright Eyes,* until tears welled in her eyes. She wondered, what did she feel about Bob? She had been so uncertain. But he was always there for her down time and she did enjoy his company. Still, there was something she could not put her finger on that prevented her from committing to him.

That was all too much to think of now. She was still numb from her father's death. After an early retirement because of Alzheimer's, he spent a few years in a nursing home before finally passing. She knew it was a merciful blessing, but felt a huge loss that she could not describe. Her father was a part of who she was, but being still young, she did not know what that meant or how his life and death effected her. She just knew that she was very sad. She would always picture herself as a small child on his lap when she thought of him. Having been his first daughter, she had held a special place in his heart. Now, she was not special in that way to anyone. Not close in that way to anyone.

And she had not reconciled these feeling with the confused, sometimes suppressed emotion caused by her father's alcoholism and violence. The family never discussed it. Mary had no place to process it.

Mary knew that somehow she had to get past this hole in her heart and the thirst for love she now felt intensely. The last semester of college was waiting for her. She needed to complete three big projects to get her degree. She did not know how she would find the energy. At this moment, she really did not even want to go back, but

could not think of anywhere else she would rather be. All
was emptiness.

Silent scream

She lit another cigarette as Viv refilled her champagne glass. The wedding was almost an hour late in getting started because the groom was nowhere to be found.

"The judge is really getting upset Mayr. He says he can't wait much longer. The good news is that the procession singers are entertaining the crowd. They are in the gazebo singing and playing guitar together. They started warming up and just got carried away."

"Well, that's good. I suppose we shouldn't wait too much longer." Mary smiled a flat smile. Her heart was screaming to her. She knew that she would need to announce the cancellation of her wedding when the judge finally decided he could not wait any longer. She put it off until then. A sip of champagne got her through the next moment.

She remembered sitting with Viv in the moonlight after her wedding shower. She surprised Viv when she asked her, "Do you think he could be the wrong guy for me?"

Viv answered, "we all have our cross to bear Mayr."

At the time she thought Viv meant that nobody's perfect. But today, one hour past the time the 200 guests seated outside expected her wedding to begin, she wondered if it might mean that going through with this wedding would mean her crucifixion. Christ knowingly went to his didn't he?

Just then, another bridesmaid came rushing into the room, bringing a steam of sunlight with her. "He is here!" Looking out the window, she could see a truck with several men in the back next to a barrel of beer. She noticed they all had cups in their hands. Her heart and soul rang together like bells that screamed an alarm she could not hear.

"Come on Mayr, let's touch up your make up and hair and get you out there. Her bridesmaids worked on her, snapped some pictures and then whisked her out to where her brother Bill stood under a tree, waiting to give her away.

Childbirth

Ringing the bell to summon the nurse, Mary emptied the last of the ice water in her carafe into her cup. Her thirst since giving birth for the first time two days ago was insatiable.

Around the corner came the nurse, very perky and loud.

"Mary, we are about to bring your baby in to your room. Can I help you get washed and ready?"

"Yes, thank you." Mary replied as she slowly crawled off the doughnut that provided little relief for the remaining pains of childbirth.

Emerging from the bathroom in a new nightgown, washed and refreshed, Mary opened the drapes to let the morning light into the room. She paused by the window to enjoy the sight of a large oak tree. It's leaves were the colors of fire still, since fall had arrived late this year. A slight breeze blew them all around. A fire dance, Mary wondered. This tree offered her a fire dance in honor of the arrival of her new son, C. Jay.

"The dinner menu is here. Be sure to fill it out. Tonight is your last night, so you will get a special dinner to share with your husband." With that, the nurse left the room to get the baby.

Mary turned from the window and carefully settled herself back on her bed. As she was pouring herself a cup of water, the nurse arrived with the baby.

"Hey, little C. Jay. Look at you all awake first thing in the morning." She lifted him from his bed and prepared to feed him. As he ate, he watched her closely, occasionally brushing her hand with his.

As she looked into his baby blue eyes, the rest of the world faded away. All that was real was this bond between mother and son. Articulated in every way except language. She sang him a lullaby to complete the moment. *All the Pretty Ponies*, sung soft and low.

"I have never seen a baby hold his head up right after he was born the way he does. This is a strong baby! Look at him eat! You two will be going home tomorrow, no problem." With that the nurse left them alone.

Mary wasn't sure that she was really ready to go home. The baby was strong and fine and a good eater. But it was painful to sit, and she still felt weak.

Bob had not returned to the hospital since the birth. He called yesterday afternoon to say he would be there for dinner last night, but never showed. Mary had been too exhausted to think too much about it last night, and turned out the lights for sleep right after dinner.

With a sigh, she filled out the dinner menu. Steak or lobster. Hmm. Get the steak. And Champaign? Why not? She wouldn't have any, but if Bob showed up, it might relax him.

She vaguely wondered what she would do if he did not show up tomorrow for her discharge. As she settled back to burp and cuddle C. Jay, she quickly composed a brief list of people to call for help before falling asleep with the baby in her arms.

She sat cross legged on a small cloud. Filled with happiness she was still, elated, serene. Somewhere within, her soul composed and orchestrated music simultaneously. Listening carefully, she could find a single emotion within each instrument. All pieces of the orchestra played endlessly the music that was her.

Below her, a steady stream of reality - people, places, things, color, light, shadows that have and will touch her. Nothing good or bad, no pain or joy beneath. All just there to view and wonder. Such power in keeping the music separate from the stream, such peace.

Pretending

As she lay in bed, in the dark, she did her best to calm her breathing. To breathe as if she was asleep. It was 3:00 AM. And Bob was pulling up in the driveway. She thought she heard him hit a garbage can in the driveway as he pulled in. Every muscle in her body was tensed. Her stomach felt rock hard and sour. God, she hated this. It took everything she had to prevent fear from overwhelming her. But she had learned from experience not to confront or argue with Bob when he was drunk. The best thing to do, was let him sleep it off and talk about it later, if he would do that. Often, he refused.

As he opened the door, she heard him stumble and swear. The thought crossed her mind that he had been with another woman. She tried desperately to dismiss it, knowing it would only interfere with her ability to survive the next several moments without violence erupting.

She heard him open the refrigerator and something glass hit the floor and shatter. When Bob did not make it home for dinner, Mary would make him a plate of food, wrap it and put it in the fridge for later. She heard a slew of obscenity before he headed down the hallway toward the bedrooms.

"Where is my little guy? Where is my C. Jay," Bob slurred loudly.

Mary tensed. If he went for the baby, as he had done in the past, she would be forced to get up and confront him. Nothing in her would allow him to wake C. Jay and handle him while drunk. She quickly said the Lords Prayer and asked for help.

The prayer seemed to work, because Bob moved into the marital bedroom, forgetting about his son. Mary went back to pretending to sleep. Focusing all of her energy into motionlessness and peacekeeping. Terrified. Sickened.

Without removing any clothing, Bob fell on the bed and instantly passed out. The smell of him overwhelmed Mary. When she was sure that he would not wake up, she moved into the nursery and gently closed the door.

She settled herself into the rocking chair and began to slowly rock. She relaxed herself by watching C. Jay sleep. She wondered what he was dreaming. Very glad that he slept through tonight's ugly scene. Deciding to think things through tomorrow, she relaxed her body by clearing all thoughts from her mind. And fell asleep in the rocker.

I haven't called you Fifi in awhile! A term of endearment from High School. It seems like such a long time ago. Yet only a moment ago.

I find myself overwhelmed with the duties of motherhood. It is as if I had to erase myself completely and then redefine myself according to the needs of this small, sweet person. Not that I'm complaining. He is such a miracle.

Rocking him is one of the most wonderful things life has to offer. Feeling him cuddle. Having him look directly into my eyes while he feeds. He drinks my eyes in completely and seems to know just what I am thinking.

Our schedule of eating, sleeping, cleaning, playing goes on around the clock. The two of us are locked into a secret society where visitors come and go but the two of us remain together always. It is an amazing feeling.

Non verbal communication on so many levels completes our responses to one another. He loves it when I read or sing, but the eye contact seems to be the most significant. And touch - can soothe or shatter the quiet (as in the case of a bad diaper rash.)

I've not felt this connection with another person ever, so real, so boundless. Surely, one of the things that makes life worth living.

I wonder if I will ever get back to writing. Motherhood seems so all consuming. I could not imagine having to go to work and leave my baby. I feel very fortunate that I will not have to make that choice.

I've read a lot of argument about whether women can write and have a family at the same time. Before I had this baby, I could not see what the fuss was all about. But now I understand that complete accessibility is what the job of motherhood demands. And writing is difficult with interruptions. How does one reconcile the two? I suppose that when I am ready, I will find a way. I hope so.

Please let me know how you are doing Viv. I love you.

mmb

I am in a bed, in a circular room with white walls holding my baby. Suddenly, half the wall moves away and opens the room up to al lush garden with trees. There is a blue bird in a pear tree singing a beautiful song.

I begin to feed my baby and a monarch butterfly lands on his cheek. He does not stop eating but looks up at me and holds my eyes with his. He has the loveliest blue eyes and I think that he is trying to tell me that he loves me. He is trying to tell me that everything will be all right. He reaches up with his little hand and rubs my cheek to confirm this.

I close my eyes and fall asleep.

Don't you hate it when they yell

C. Jay cuddled up next to her on the car seat after his grandmother left the car to get everyone drinks from McDonald's. She put her arms around her son and thought how glad she was to get away from home for the day to go shopping with her mom.

Bob had been angry and moody lately, not wanting to talk about what might be bothering him but complaining and arguing about everything under the sun. She sighed and kissed the top of the little blonde head beneath her.

"Don't you hate it when they yell at you?" C. Jay's question made her laugh. It was just like him to read her thoughts and give a sympathetic comment out of the blue. He had been doing it since he could first speak. What a wonderful child. What a deep, heartfelt connection between them.

"Well don't you two look happy and cozy," said her mother as she sat back in the driver's seat.

"Yea, when will you be installing a rocking chair in here for good family love? Now that you have so many grandchildren, you need one!"

"Well, we wouldn't want you to get too comfortable, we would never be able to get you to go home." Her mom gave her a searching look. She probably knew there was trouble on the home front, but was not really one to discuss it.

"Hey, if we don't leave nicely you won't come back, we know that," Mary teased. "Come on, pass those drinks please. I am sooooo thirsty."

"Me too, I'm soooooo thirsty," chimed C. Jay. Ever the sympathetic buddy.

I am walking through a café. Quickly, unexplainably, I ask for coffee to go. The man next to me begins to scream at me – cold, abusive, cruel accusations. I run for the door, but duck down an isle and hide. I see him running out the door after me. Momentary relief.

I go and speak to the owner and we are both glad of my trick. I begin to walk out of the door but am suddenly afraid. I run towards the back of the café and find a dark room to hide in. As my eyes grow accustom to the dark, I see the figure of the lunatic man sitting in a chair before me. Simultaneously, I hear the café being locked and left for the evening.

My fear dissipates. I decide to help this crazy man with understanding and emotion. I talk to him at length. I touch him. He cries and I comfort him with my arms and heart. We make love and marry.

I find myself working in his apartment. He is out. I suddenly become frightened and get up to lock the door. While my hand is on the lock a woman burst in. Her name is Karen. She raves that she is my husbands wife and that she will kill him. I tell her that what she is saying is impossible, yet remember that he told me to set up a studio for myself in Karen's room. I tell her this and she screams "Karen's room, Karen's room," over and over.

I run to the bedroom and find him sleeping, hidden by the covers, dressed in candy striped pajamas. He wakes and I run through the apartment, through rooms that weren't there before. There is a man in one room laughing at me, laughing insanely. I run back to my husband and he tells me that we will have to put Karen in the closet. I tell him this is insane, that she is a human being.

Karen enters and all three, Karen, my husband and the insane laughing man walk toward me, grab me and put me in the closet. I feel myself relaxing in their grasp, and wake up.

I want to be a werewolf

What a great Mother's Day! She joined forces with one
of her favorite families that included three children
around the same age as C. Jay and tracked everyone down
to the Second City Theater to see their Sunday children's
show. She and Bob had taken C. Jay many times but they
had never included friends. The sun was shining, the air
was fresh and she felt wonderfully happy.

One of the other children rode with them in her car and
they chatted all the way downtown, leaving the driving to
Bob. The children were as excited as she was about the
Mother's Day plans, dinner and a show downtown. The
Second City children's shows were always hilarious and
never condescended to the children. Very heady, silly
stuff for kids.

The afternoon flew past as they laughed themselves to
tears, hugged and cuddled in the audience. At the end of
the show, one of the comedians came out for an
interactive discussion with the children. "What do you
want to be when you grow up?" she asked, encouraging
them to call out their secret desires.

She looked over at C. Jay and smiled. He looked back at
her, connected completely for a moment, then stood on
his chair and yelled "I WANT TO BE A WEREWOLF!"

He immediately threw his arms around her as she burst
out laughing. Catching her off balance, she laughed
herself right off her chair, taking him to the floor with
her. There, they had a good long laugh before even
attempting to get back up.

Nobody's brother

Denny's was probably her least favorite restaurant, but it had been C. Jay's choice. It was the first time in the Christmas season that they had gone shopping together. They were both happy and excited. Now that C. Jay was four, he was great company, very articulate, lots of questions, already highly developed sense of humor, wonderfully abstract thinker.

She looked up from her menu ready to ask C. Jay what he wanted to eat when she saw him all slumped down, head hanging so very sadly.

"Cj, what's up buddy," she asked as she gave his little back a rub.

"I'm nobody's brother," he cried with a tone that broke her heart to pieces.

Looking around quickly she spotted two brothers in the booth across playing and laughing.

"Well, you know that could change at any time. You never told me that you wanted to be somebody's brother. When did you start feeling this way?"

"I don't know. Everyone has a brother or sister but me!"

She reflected on all of the times her mom told her that she had seven children because as an only child, she decided that no other child should be that lonely. It seems that she was right. With all the uncertainty in her marriage her concern was not bringing another child into

---

that chaos. She hadn't considered that C. Jay might just need someone, or that he wanted to be an older brother.

"You know, babies cry. And little brothers or sisters can be very pesky!"

He sat up and began to play again. "I don't care. I just want to be somebody's brother. I think I would want a brother."

"What if you got a sister instead?"

"Well, I guess that would be OK too."

She thought of his friend Sharon in her family full of sisters. She could see that C. Jay would be a wonderful older brother to a girl or boy.

"Well, I guess we'll need to get to work on that! But it won't happen by Christmas! Let's talk about presents we want to find today." Bells rang as a group of carolers began to sing *"Silent Night"* in the restaurant. Mother and son laughed.

As C. Jay stood up in the booth and put his arms around her, she embraced the light of joy in his eyes. "I know. Thanks mom."

"Can I take your order?" She turned to the waitress with tears in her eyes and replied "I think we need a moment, thanks"

Ten months later, C. Jay rode home from the hospital singing *the ABC song* to his new brother Toby in the back seat.

Dear Vivi,

Oh, Viv – I hit the black hole of motherhood. This lovely, perfect, new child of mine, at only three weeks old, developed colic. Not just a little crying here or there. Twelve hours of intense screaming daily. He switches back and forth between day and night. I don't know which is worse. If he cries during the day I can't do anything else but care for him. If he cries at night I get no sleep because of all the things to be done during the day. The pediatrician told me not to worry, he had never seen a case last longer than six months.

Well, it seems this cherub was born to set records. It has been six months and two weeks. And, like the Energizer bunny, he keeps going and going. Twelve friggin hours out of twenty four. Poor little guy. What a way to enter the world. It is as if a valve shuts and he can pass no gas. Then it opens again and he burps and everything else like clockwork. He is so loving, cuddly and beautiful when he is not in such pain that he is rigid with screaming.

I have tried driving him in the car as recommended, but it doesn't help him and certainly doesn't help anyone else on the road in my path. Nerve wracked driver must be worse than a drunk driver. The upside is no one would dare ticket me.

I walk the halls every night in the dark, bouncing him on my hip or shoulder. If I put him down his cries intensify. Well, I guess I would not want to go through it alone either. So it's Toby and me facing it together.

Bob and C. Jay take off as much as possible and I don't blame them a bit. Poor C. Jay, when he hears one of his friends say they want their mom to have a baby he tells them emphatically, " YOU DO NOT WANT A BABY."

I don't think he believes there will be an end to it any more than I do. We are locked into the eternal primal scream. I feel an incredible, deep love for this child. When the crying starts, the love increases. And we are bonded in the noise and the anguish. Walking, singing, waiting for it all to end.

Yesterday, I put my rocking chair by the picture window so that I could see the sun rise through the trees while we rocked through the scream. Bob came in the room and I asked him, "What would you do if you came home one day and I was catatonic?

He said, "face you toward the TV so that you had something to watch." Funny guy. He left quickly after that to get away from the noise.

Well I am sure we will make it through. Pretty sure any way. If you don't get an answer when you call, freak out! Cos I'm surely not going anywhere. And I am up around the clock.

I am hoping that because the infancy has been so rough, this little tiger will bless me with an easy adolescence. What do you think my chances are?

Your favorite zombie,

mmb

I have this dream once or twice a week, ever since Toby was born. So much anxiety, almost terror runs through it. Somewhere in the dream, usually at different times, in different rooms, I realize that it is a dream that I have had many times before. But this does not ease the anxiety. It increases the need to find my son more than ever.

I walk into the nursery and find Toby missing. I know he is somewhere. I know he needs me. He is in some kind of trouble or distress and is calling for me, somewhere so far that I cannot hear him. But I know it. Magnetic ABC letters are all over the nursery floor. They hurt my feet when I step on them but I don't care. I search the crib for Toby's binky. If he has his binky, wherever he is, at least he can calm himself. I find the binky next to his favorite bear. I pick up both and run from the room calling his name.

I run to the living room. It is dark. The rocking chair is rocking.

"Toby," I call, running over to the chair. The chair is empty. I turn on the light and look down at my legs. They are covered in bruises. My arms have many bruises too. This alarms me further. I grab a coat and run out of the house to the neighbors.

The neighbors house is a dream house. It is the same house in every one of these dreams. But it is not actually one of my neighbor's homes.

The first room of the house has only a piano. It is playing itself, a tune that a child would create banging on the piano for fun. There are three women dancing around the piano.

"Where is Toby? I have to find him. He needs me."

The dancing women laugh. They laugh and dance to the piano music.

I run to the next room. I run over to a fire place. A child is resting on a pillow in front of a beautiful fire. When I reach the child, I see that it is not Toby.

"Do you know where Toby is?" Then I notice the child has headphones on. He does not hear me. This upsets me so much I try to scream. No sound will come from my throat. I try and try, but my scream is silent. In tears, I run from this room to the next.

In the next room there are Christmas lights all over. Silent Night is playing on a radio. As I look more closely at the lights, I see that many of the bulbs are broken. This terrifies me for some reason. I turn to run out of the room and see a young girl whose hands are outstretched to me. I kneel down and she slowly walks over to me but says nothing. In her hand I see many pieces of broken pencil. Terrified, I jump up and run from the house.

As I run out the front door I see a picture of Toby that crashes to the floor before I can catch it.

I run through the woods calling Toby. People in Halloween costumes jump out from behind the trees and try to scare me.

I keep running through the woods to the beach, calling Toby's name as I run. I run and run, but never lose my breath. The running relieves my anxiety. When I reach the beach I stop to look at the reflection of the moon and the stars on the water. From behind me, Toby calls, "Mom."

As I turn he runs toward me. He jumps into my arms and says "Mom, I love you."

I wake, shaking and crying, sometimes yelling. The sound of his voice is always still in my ears. It is always the same. But in waking life, my son cannot yet speak.

Family Weekends

Mary reached for the diaper bag that was leaning under the tree and grabbed the binky. Toby had fallen and was crying more from anger and frustration than pain. He so wanted to keep up with the older kids, his little body just would not cooperate.

She scooped him up, brushed him off, sat him on her lap and handed him the binky. The pacifier was his way to self soothe, just as it had been hers. This she could understand in the deepest part of herself. She kept it clean and handy for just such occasions.

A group of children ran by laughing. Toby quickly took a drink of water and handed Mary the binky. Then he was off and running.

Mary loved these family weekends. Her family was so large that she was invited to some kind of get together every weekend. This was Shawn and Pat's annual summer get together to celebrate July 4th and all the birthdays surrounding it.

Meg sat down next to Mary as soon as Toby took off.

"Hey Mayr. Is Bob going to make it?"

"Doubt it. He usually works Saturdays. But he will be at Maeve's tomorrow. No work on Sunday. That is the rule. After that, I don't complain. As long as the kids and I have one day a week. Are you going tomorrow?"

Meg passed Mary a handful of pictures from their get together last weekend at her house. "Yep, but I'll be late. We have to stop at my in-laws first."

"Are your weekends filled up with family like mine are? It is a good thing I don't work. It leaves the rest of the week for the boys and I to see the world outside of this family."

Meg chuckled. "There is a great picture of Bob pouring a beer on his head."

Mary passed the pictures back to Meg without looking at them. "You should stick to taking pictures of the children. We don't need reminders of how idiotic the adults can be."

"Come on now, it was late, you know."

"Please, don't make excuses. I had to smell that all the way home."

"Mom, come on, play ball with us," yelled C. Jay from across the yard.

"Finally, the voice of sanity," cried Mary as she ran over to the children to play basketball.

Time to give back

Bells chimed as Toby banged out a tune on his little synthesizer. No matter how many times Mary hid that toy, her son managed to find it. She wished she had the heart to throw it away but she knew he loved to bang away on it with all the different sounds it could make.

A commercial came on the TV. A beautiful image of light streaming through trees in a park where children played. Another commercial on volunteerism. There seemed to be a lot of them lately. Or was she just finally receptive to the idea.

Toby was scheduled to start nursery school in the fall. It was the same cooperative nursery school that C. Jay had attended. Mary could only fulfill the minimum required adult participation during C. Jay's enrollment because Toby was at home with colic and then teething. It had been her zombie phase.

But now, while Toby was in class two or three mornings a week, she would have time to volunteer. And she was ready to be involved with the schools. She believed in the idea of giving back.

The nursery school asked her to be president of the board of directors and she had agreed, thinking it was time to pay her dues. It was the job no one wanted but she accepted it gladly.

C. Jay's school was in need of a PTA committee chairman for the Child Health and Welfare Committee. After asking around, Mary found out that this committee was in the process of bringing an alcohol and other drug prevention program to the school called CLOWN

(Children Learning Other Ways Naturally.) She chose this over directing the talent show or fun fair because she welcomed the opportunity to find out how to talk to kids about these issues.

As her children grew, Mary had become concerned about them seeing adults drunk at family get togethers. Bob caved in to her moderate use philosophy when C. Jay was born and allowed parenting to take the place of partying. Frankly, this had saved their marriage. But occasionally, he fell off the wagon and it always created tension between them.

Mary watched her children watching people who had too much to drink with curiosity and concern. They would often crawl on to her lap and become the Velcro children.

So, she considered taking this position with the primary school PTA an everyone wins situation. The school would get a volunteer willing to do the work necessary to bring effective prevention programs into the district. Mary would learn how to talk to her children about these sensitive issues.

"Come on mom, dance to the music," Toby said with a laugh as he broke into her thoughts. As she danced her silly dance around the room to his unusual music, she silently wished that this joy of motherhood would never end.

Beach day

C. Jay ran over to her and arrived out of breath. He had been watching the same spectacle she had, children riding their bicycles off the pier, into the water. Some would build their speed before the plunge by starting from the top of the sledding hill on the other side of the playground, then over the pier and out into the water. The hill certainly afforded them a terrific flight before their swim.

"Mom, what do you think?"

"It sure looks like fun doesn't it?"

"Yea, can I go home and get my bike?"

"Sure, but I don't think it is very good for their bikes. Getting bikes all wet like that takes all the grease and oil off the places that need it. Those bikes might rust a lot sooner too. If you do that, we will have to take your bike in right away for service so it will still race well for you."

"Still race well. Mom, you sure have a way with words." But his face had fallen with his shoulders. His evaporating dream had deflated them. She felt for him.

"You'll just have to invent some better fun."

With that he went to the lake's bank and sat on a bench. His friend Amanda joined him shortly after. She watched the two of them. She loved them both dearly, yet they were so very different. They were twelve now. But when they were together, they both changed a little, gained something wonderful, had some kind of usness between them. She hadn't noticed this with any other girl. She began to revel in what the future might hold for C. Jay.

"Look at them, I didn't know C. Jay talked to girls." Amanda's mother Donna and Mary's neighbor Kate were shifting their chairs closer to Mary's so that they could enjoy the moment together. Donna had been the first friend that Mary made at the children's nursery school years ago. Mary had been impressed with the way that she walked right up and introduced herself. They had a long discussion that day, who knows about what? Didn't matter. The friendship was sealed then and there.

It was Donna, Kate and Mary's once a week schedule of getting all the kids together to play that led to the Beach Day tradition. They got tired of the planning and calling and organizing involved. The private beach on this beautiful spring fed lake was just a block from Mary's home. So as soon as, and as long as, the weather was warm enough, they met at the beach each Wednesday.

Mary usually began the season before most other families, because Toby would swim in the lake while there was still ice on it. She had to keep a life jacket on him all summer until he was old enough to get swimming lessons at the local YMCA. He was a water baby. The beach was his spot of comfort. So she went with it. And built a fire in the barbecue for warmth on those days.

The group started small in the early years and grew. Mary requested parking permits from the Park District for her guests. She took all permits that were available that day, declaring her group as the Wildwood Parent Network. Her neighbor Suzanne eventually joined the group because her son Tom was always there with C. Jay.

As each summer progressed, she would hear children in the neighborhood proclaiming "It's Beach Day." More and more children and parents participated. It became a time when everyone knew they could catch up with their friends and neighbors. Occasionally, a dad would take off of work to join in the fun. Sometimes they barbecued lunch. Sometimes a family would dock their boat or bring a para-sail.

But even without anything fancy, the day was perfect with friends and family, relaxation and happiness. Some sat in the shade of the trees. Some never went into the water. Everyone could be themselves. Although there were times that the "beach patrol" (whoever was willing to get up and yell) would need to calm the kids down before someone got hurt.

There were Beach Days that C. Jay and Toby wanted to begin with breakfast. Extra coolers were needed to make sure there was enough to eat and drink for the day. Some days, the children would not leave until sunset, and Mary had no will to disagree. It was wonderful to watch the changing light of the sunset on beach scene. Even though they lived only one block from this beach, they rarely went home for anything on beach day. It was perfect in and of itself. Many of the supplies needed were just left in the trunk of the car until next week.

"I think I am enjoying my children's childhood almost as much as my own. If you cut out all of the family squabbles and life troubles, this is a great way to grow up. I hope my children always remember the peace and joy of Beach Day - along with tree jumping at Pebble Beach, ice hockey on the lake in the winter, sledding on the local hills, climbing trees, bonfires, you know, all that stuff."

"They will," Donna said as she patted her friends hand, "They will remember."

I found a picture yesterday at my mom's that I must tell you about. I am probably about four or five because I look very much like your beloved kindergarten picture of me that you like to show everyone. I am surrounded by my four brothers. We are all dressed for church or some other dress occasion and standing in front of a fire place. The boys have sport coats and ties. I have a skirt and blouse and my hair has been curled. Dressy for me - I was a wannabe tomboy.

The boys are all looking so suave and debonair. I am leaning against a chair with my cheek to it. What is it we were asked to pose for, a teen magazine? GQ? How did we have such grown up expectations back then?

I realized by looking at this picture that growing up surrounded by four brothers had definite effects on me. Brought about my need to please - so that I could be included. Created a comfort with intimacy that does not involve sexual feelings. This has gotten me in trouble over the years because most of men can only associate intimacy with sex. Can or want to, I am not sure which.

Anyway, because my dad gave me a lot of physical affection, I in turn gave that to my brothers who received it gladly. I grew up kissing them on the lips hello and goodbye, leaning on them when sitting next to them, holding hands while walking, hugging a lot. This natural affection has also created a lot of trouble for me with men as you can imagine.

It is the need to please that I am having the hardest time with. That fear of being shut out. The need to be included. The willingness to do anything to please and maintain intimacy. I am sure my brothers took advantage of that when we were little, with no understanding of how that might drown me later.

I would like to be able to be so self contained and self assured that I can be happy whether or not I am pleasing anyone (especially men.) I tell myself that I just need to do my best and not worry about who it is pleasing. But this script runs very deep and I find myself falling into it at the most surprising times. When I realize I am doing it a mirror flashes in my mind. The reflection is not a pretty one.

I have been wondering a lot about internal scripts lately. Any insights?

mmb

I am sitting on a beach watching the waves go in and out.
I pick up the sand and pour it from hand to hand. I feel
drained, as if I just began to recover from a long illness.
The only sound is the waves on the shore.

Suddenly, a big crow lands on the sand next to me. I
look right into his little black eyes to try to discover his
intention. He stares right back at me and remains silent.

Backyard heaven

Mary rang the bell fastened to the house by the door to call the children to lunch. This bell had been a cherished Christmas gift from her mother. Her mom thought it would stop her from sounding like a shrew when she called the children. Her mom was right!

Carrying pitchers of ice water and juice to the picnic table, she noticed more children than usual sitting down to lunch.

"Looks like we will have to put more hot dogs on the grill," she said with a smile.

"We have some at home, I'll go get them!" And with that one of the neighborhood children ran off.

Mary knew that some of her neighbors were teachers, and their school year ended after their children's school year. This left some of these children home alone for a few days while mom was at work. It was good that they found their way to her yard. She was glad to care for them, feeling fortunate that she was able to stay home full time with her family.

The picnic table filled quickly as she passed around cups and chips. It was a noisy group of boys and girls that seemed to come from all directions.

Usually, this backyard heaven was filled with ten or so boys from the neighborhood. Toby was always the youngest but age did not seem to matter. Suzanne and Kate's boys were usually among the group. Today there were many more than the usual ten. Those who couldn't get a seat on the picnic table sat on the patio bench or the tire swing.

"Where did you all come from?" Mary probed to find out this mornings game.

"We are building a bike track with a ramp in the woods," explained C. Jay.

Next to their home was four, wooded, vacant lots. This piece of land became the neighborhood playground for fort building and bike riding. Mary's yard had a big sand pit for the younger children, and a big tire swing for the older ones. Mary affectionately called the swing, "the child eater."

When Mary asked Bob to put up a tire swing, she hadn't expected the semi-truck tire with plastic coated chains that swung the entire width of her yard and attracted children like a ride at an amusement park. He climbed the highest, biggest tree in the yard to hang the swing. She was shocked and delighted.

After composing safety rules and drilling them into the children she crossed her fingers, held her breath and hoped that an occasional sick stomach was the worst injury to be seen. The children quickly learned their limits, although she often had to walk away, not able to watch as they spun in circles until they were sick.

Sometimes, she would bring her coffee outside, put a saucer sled inside the tire and lay in the swing, gently swaying in the breeze. Looking up at the trees and thinking about how motherhood suited her even though her marriage was a nightmare. She learned to shut out the pain of her marriage and enjoy watching her sons grow.

The children scattered as she began to clean off the picnic table. She had not been this happy since she was a child playing in the woods. Whatever the future brought, she hoped this feeling would never end.

The precipice

She squirmed in her chair in the counselor's office.

"There is such a thing as fair fighting. You two don't
have a clue about what that means. The truth is, this is a
place for people who are willing to admit they have an
addiction to alcohol or drugs, and want to do something
to treat that addiction. From everything I have heard
here, I don't think this is the place for you. Why don't
you try marital counseling."

This cheered Bob up tremendously. "I told you. We
don't belong here. I don't have a problem with alcohol."

The counselor paused, looked directly at Mary and then
spoke slowly.

"For us to help you, Bob will need to admit that he has a
problem. He just told us that he is not going to do that.
You two definitely need some help, but we can't give it to
you. Let me recommend a counselor. He is one of the
best. I hope he can help."

Mary looked over at Bob who was obviously still feeling
triumphant. There was a puzzle. She could not help but
wonder what he understood and what he was thinking.
Mary had given him an ultimatum, get help for excessive
drinking or get out. She had the distinct feeling he now
thought he was off the hook.

They were quiet all the way to the car before Mary said
anything. She stood by the driver's door looking into
Bob's eyes.

"I will give this counselor a try. But I will not live with the drinking anymore, or the name calling, or the fighting. If we can turn this around with a counselor, that will be great. I think we owe it to the children to try. But I want to be perfectly clear. I will not live the way we have been living while we try counseling." She crossed her arms and shivered in the cold.

"Come on Mayr, get in the car, we'll talk on the way home."

They did talk on the way home. But Mary felt uneasy. She felt (like always) as if she was being told what she wanted to hear. And she was not at all certain if they would be able to work through these problems. She did know that she was not going to raise her children with a raving drunk in the house. She would not put up with the constant beating on her self esteem caused by his belittling and game playing. She wondered how long she could go on. She wondered how she would be able to start over on her own, if she had to. She wondered what would happen to her children in the process.

With a heavy sigh, she left the silence in the car undisturbed for the rest of the ride home. The car was silent, but her thoughts were screaming.

Picture this: a girl is taught that love is forever. She expects, because of her strong religious upbringing, that marriage is forever. That she must do everything she can to work it out. She truly believes that all of this will make her happy. Keeping her family together is the right thing. Children's having two parents together is the right thing.

The twin picture to this is the unseen control that crept into her life. The realization hit her like a freight train. Unseen control woven into every fiber of her daily life.

Lies. Sometimes ridiculous lies! Told to control the outcome. Told to control the emotion. Told to control psychologically.

Sabotage. As she gets close to a victory, a personal success, he orchestrates a crisis to prevent it. He is so tuned into her personal happiness, this comes naturally. Everything implied, denied. It has happened so many times that it is now perfected. And in her life, it is expected. But she usually blames her self, throwing her into self loathing and discouragement.

If, by chance, the promise of a victory slips by him, and she is able to bask in the glory – he becomes cold, remote, and almost angry. But not angry enough to arouse suspicion. Of course, she is so happy just to have a small victory, she doesn't suspect a thing.

He encouraged her to quit school before finishing. He promised to take care of her in her grief. Promised it would be alright, assured her that it was the right thing to do. Painted a bright future with his pallet of lies and broken promises. And through her grief, she never saw the real picture.

She ends relationships because of his constant interference. He would make a pass at a friend who was drunk (he was pouring.) He would endlessly belittle the people she loved to her. If none of that worked, his rage would frighten them away. And increase her isolation.

When did he begin to refuse to go with her to see her family? Find other, more important things for them to be doing? All the while, developing relationships with them secretly, alone, without her.

Blame. She became the blame vortex. And he became blame's primary natural resource. Blame surrounds her like the wind on a winter day, relentlessly howling. She would resist until her thirst for peace drove her to acceptance. Peace at all cost. Exhausted, she would allow the short peace to heal her. Until he sensed it was time for more. Sensed it was time to maintain control.

Along with blame, and after the acceptance, always came the push. Push away. The passive aggressive silence. The punishment. And then, lest he lose control, when the time was right, more blame. Why are you always over there? Why do you do this to us? She was blamed for accepting the blame. Round and round they go.

All of the stress brings illness. For which of course, she blames herself. Probably just to avoid having the blame used as a weapon. She blames herself to avoid the pain of being blamed by him. As soon as she becomes ill, he disappears. Finds a reason to leave town. Or comes home for only a few hours a night, while the family sleeps. No support, only absence, isolation.

She does not see, until it was too late, that he hovered over her every move. That she had no room to be herself, without him. She did not understand this, until it was impossible for her. Only by leaving the marriage, would she ever have her independence. No, he needed her to be completely dependent. None of these tricks would work otherwise.

She was taught to stay and work it out. Her parents had done this in their own way. Her mother told her she stayed in her unhappy marriage because she thought it was best for her children. But she also taught Mary never to let a man hit her. To leave immediately.

Yes, violence was the last, most insidious form of unseen control in her life. And as she began to understand all of the forms violence could take, she began to wonder at her mothers advice. How could her mother ignore the fact that Bill was beaten, yet tell her to leave if she was ever hit. Her mother did not understand the violence in her life either.

In Mary's life violence took many forms. Violence, when in a rage, he threw her things around the house or out the door. The violence in taking her food away and demanding she leave the dinner table when he did not like a comment. The violence in physically blocking her way with his body, so that she could not pass by him. The violence in the constant belittling, the violence in removing her access to the family accounts, screaming so close to her face, all unseen control.

Now, she is stuck, sitting in a chair constructed from her confusion. Can she stay and work it out? Is it possible for someone this violent to see himself clearly? Can these problems be solved? Is the damage done to the heart and minds of the children worth staying to work it out? Here, she will remain seated until she can find the strength to stand.

These twin pictures bear no resemblance to each other. But together, create the moral dilemma I now face. Everyone has a different opinion. Everyone sees it differently. I know that I will have to find the answer somewhere inside myself. The self so cluttered and disguised by unseen control that finding anything seems impossible.

My children keep me going day to day. Their bright faces, their capacity for joy, make life worth living daily. As I search my soul for the answer to my moral dilemma.

Love,

mmb

I am in a house of mirrors, running. Frightened and running. In each real and distorted image is my body running – and my husband's face laughing. Laughing at my flight. No, not laughing, crying. No, you are not crying. My images in the mirrors are crying. His face expresses no emotion after the laughter stops. No emotion, not one. Not in one image. Not one. Not any. And I crumble into blindness.

Suzanne's counsel

Mary could tell that her neighbor Suzanne was deep in thought after what she just told her. Spontaneously, Mary told Suzanne that she and Bob had been in counseling for several months before her surgery.

Now, Suzanne was giving her a ride to her OBGYN for her follow up exam after an emergency hysterectomy. Mary began bleeding uncontrollably last month and this surgery, she was told, was life saving. But the doctors could not give her a reason for her condition. It was suggested that the problem could have been stress related, but no how or why was offered.

Mary confided to Suzanne that she was at the end of her rope with counseling. It did not seem to be resolving her marital problems and now she was concerned about the effect of her failing marriage on her health.

Suzanne broke the revere, "Why not try a different counselor?"

"Different how?" asked Mary.

"Well, my husband and I are seeing a counselor that also sees me separately. He is a marital counselor and a psychotherapist. Both of you might benefit from psychotherapy. It has helped me figure myself out."

"I mean, let's face it Mary, are you prepared to end your marriage? Give your self some time to recover from the surgery. And in the meantime, this guy might be able to help you."

Mary tried to picture herself on her own. It would be awhile before she could get a job. Three months, according to the doctors. She closed her eyes and let the darkness comfort her. She knew she did not have the energy to end her marriage now.

"Thanks, I'll think about that. Sometimes it pays off to tell your secrets. Thank you."

Suzanne laughed, "I know what you mean. I haven't told anyone else that I'm seeing a counselor. It took me a few minutes to get up the courage to tell you. But I am glad I did. I know I can trust you."

"Thanks, you are a good pal."

Smashing Christmas

She stared at the wall, feeling none of the cheer the
Christmas season usually brought. This Christmas was
just one to be endured. Bob was having a long, angry,
silent spell. He would not discuss presents for the
children. It was two days before Christmas and they still
did not have a tree. Mary secretly applied to the local
township for assistance so that she could give the
children a Christmas dinner and a few gifts if nothing
else.

She saw the strain each day on her children. The
Christmas season was usually filled with shopping, baking
gingerbread, making gingerbread houses, parties. This
year, the absence of all that weighed more heavily each
day on their little hearts.

She became aware of a noise, what was that? Tap and
shatter, tap and shatter. She listened closely but could not
define it. Motherly instinct brought her to her feet and
took her out into the cold to see what was going on.

Toby came out from behind the car in the driveway,
hammer in hand.

"What are you doing, baby?"

He ran up to the garden, where Mary laid the Christmas
lights yesterday, and began to smash the lights with a
hammer. Mary stood, stunned and speechless.

Yesterday, Toby begged her to put out the Christmas
lights. In the past, Bob put up the lights with the children
as part of the season festivities. Mary did not even know
where they were kept. But Toby found them and pleaded

with Mary to help him put them up. Today, he was smashing them, one by one, with a hammer that looked very big in his little hands.

Mary quietly waited for him to finish. Suddenly, Bob ran out of the garage screaming. Mary had no idea that he was in there and jumped over next to Toby in fright. Toby stopped the destruction and leaned on Mary's leg.

"What the hell is going on here? This is dangerous. Clean up this glass."

"Why don't we ask Toby why he is breaking the lights?"

"Don't be an idiot. Give me that hammer. Clean up this mess before someone gets hurt."

"Funny that you should worry about that now. Could it be that what hurts is the absence of Christmas? What are you going to contribute this year? Or will you just sit by and enjoy all the suffering.?"

"Shut up you bitch."

With that Bob stormed back into the garage and slammed the door. Mary sat down on the front step and Toby sat next to her, resting his head on her lap. She quietly stroked his cheek for awhile. When she felt them both shivering from the cold, she suggested they go inside for hot chocolate.

"Come on baby, we will clean this up a little later."

Another Mom to work

Across the desk from her, sat the Director of Youth Services at the local township. Mary knew him from her volunteer work at the children's school. It was the director that hooked her up with some money and food last Christmas when things looked so dim. Mary was not sure why she was asked to this meeting, and began to move around in her chair to feel comfortable.

"Mary, I will be direct. You need a job. I know how difficult your marriage has been. I know you can use the money. You have been working as a volunteer for the past six years doing an outstanding job. Come and work for me at the township in Youth Services. I can start you out part time. The hours will be completely flexible and if you need to, you can certainly bring your children to the township while you work."

Mary felt herself grow quiet and still. This was more than she hoped for. A job offer within walking distance from home, that would accommodate her children entirely.

Toby and C. Jay grew up playing at the township park. Participating in the sports, football, baseball, basketball and tennis. They were perfectly comfortable here. If Mary had to go to work, this would be an ideal way to gentle them into it. They could always reach her and be with her. Working part time at first would allow her to see them off to school and be home when they got there after school. For awhile anyway.

As if the director had been reading her thoughts, he added, "during the summer, you can work from home instead of coming to the office here. With the summers here, this is a busy place. It would be better for us if you worked from home too."

A light went on in Mary's mind. This was certainly something that interested her. The best part of this: her children would continue to benefit from the work she was doing in their community.

"Tell me more about the programs you have in place currently and what you envision."

Mary tried to subdue her emotion so that she could hear and remember all that was said. That was difficult, because her heart was screaming: Thank You!

I am walking down a highway. There are no cars. It is no particular time of day, but it is daytime. There is a thick rope in the shape of a noose around my neck but it doesn't bother me. It hangs down my chest like a necklace.

I keep walking for miles, as if walking were my only purpose. I don't think of anything else but walking. I am not feeling anything really not happy, not sad, no feeling really. After walking for a long time, I wake up.

I was offered a job recently and am seriously considering rejoining the workforce. Reluctantly so. I loved staying home and being completely accessible to my children. I loved sharing their childhood in ways that my parents were not able to share mine. I love seeing the world through their eyes in ways that only sharing time can give us.

But it is time. Things just keep getting worse in my marriage and I need to begin to take steps out.

I wish this was an exciting beginning, not a painful one. I want to look at it like a new beginning and recognize all of the promise beginnings hold.

Remember when we watched the sunset over the ocean, counting the seal families as they swam by? We stayed well after dark, not wanting the moment between us to end. We talked for hours about the promise of life and the possibilities before us. The sound of the water on the shore line provided the rhythm of our conversation. The changing light colored our ideas for us. The fires after dark provided the inspiration for our brain storm. Wouldn't it be great if every beginning possessed so much wonder, such love?

mmb

Time to end it

"Township Youth Services, may I help you?"

"Hi Mary. I'm sorry it took a few days to get back to you. I was out of town at a conference. How is everything?"

Mary took a deep breath before beginning. Her counselor seemed to be in a very good mood. She wondered if he was prepared for what she was about to say.

"Thanks for calling me back. I need to set up an appointment to bring the children in with me. Things have gotten very bad since my release from the hospital. I need to end it. I would like your help with the children."

Her counselor let out a long heavy sigh. Then through the silence on the line, she thought she heard him crying.

Well, it had been a long hard road together. For almost two years they had been going round and around in marriage counseling. Things got progressively worse, even violent. Out of desperation, Mary began calling the women's shelter crisis line. Every person she talked to from the shelter advised her to end the marriage. They even gave her referrals for legal advise.

Just as she was about to call the attorney, she was suddenly stricken with Strep Pneumonia. One day, she felt like she had a cold at her son's football games, the next they were draining her lungs trying to save her life. Amazing that she could get so sick within 24 hours.

Her hospital stay lasted ten days. During that time, her counselor called her, frantic because Bob left him a message stating only that she was in the hospital. She recalled his relief ,"Oh Mayr, I thought he…I thought you…I'm sorry to hear it is such a terrible illness, but glad to hear you will be OK."

"I know what you thought. We do need to talk about the possibility that the violence at home will land me here. Let's not continue to ignore that."

"No, we won't ignore it. You get better and see me when you can."

Well, talking did not stop things from escalating. Bob was full of rage after she came home from the hospital. A couple of times, the rage became physical.

The doctors, again, suggested that the stress from her marriage was effecting her health. The counselor had no answers and there seemed to be no stopping the escalating violence. Yes, it was time to end it.

Feeling terribly thirsty, she grabbed the bottle of water on her desk. The silence on the phone gave her time for a good long drink and more reflection.

Even their Catholic Priest told her she was making the right choice after witnessing Bob's rage in church, to the humiliation of the children. Last month, Bob began screaming at her that she was a terrible mother and had no place in the church during a first communion rehearsal. The priest tried to counsel Bob but got nowhere. His solution was to bless Mary, absolve her from all sin, and recommend divorce.

She had a job. She and the children would be fine. It was time. Mary knew that this counselor had done everything he possibly could to help. And he watched her try everything she possibly could to make the marriage work. All to no avail. That was a good reason for tears. Though Mary had none.

The counselor whispered "Excuse me," blew his nose, and then they scheduled an appointment. She would take the children in so that she could tell them that she was filing for divorce in the supportive atmosphere of the counselor's office. She would recommend that Bob come too. She had no idea whether or not he would come. She no longer recognized him.

Sole Custody

The phone rang as she zipped in and out of lanes in rush hour traffic.

"This is Mary," was the way she always answered her car phone. She never knew if the call was business or personal on this number.

"Hi Mary. I'm sorry that I didn't get back to you sooner, but it took me quite some time to finally connect with your husband." It was her attorney.

"Oh good, did he agree to sharing an attorney and joint custody?"

"No, I think he is going to get his own attorney. I know you wanted to end this in the kindest, quickest way possible, but it doesn't look like that will happen."

She waited for him to continue before saying, "Well, what did he say?"

After a heavy sigh, "He is going to file for sole custody."

"What does that mean?"

Well, he assumes that you won't have anything to do with the children after the divorce."

"Why would he think that?

"I don't know. But he will be getting his own attorney. Since he is filing for sole custody, you need to do the same. In the end, since you both want to stay in the children's lives, you will probably get joint custody."

"I don't understand. If that is the expected result, why don't we just agree to that in the beginning?"

"Well, all I can say is that your husband, at this time, is not agreeable. He is determined to file for sole custody. That really leaves you no alternative but to do the same. That's where we need to begin."

"How does he expect to get sole custody? I am a good mom. I teach parenting classes! I don't understand how he can do that!"

"He can file any motion that he wants to, he is their father. If you two can't come to an agreement, the court will make the decisions. You are a good mom. He will not be able to take your children away. Don't worry about that. But this isn't going to be easy. He wants to fight."

"Well, thank you. Will you represent me?"

"Yes, yes of course."

"OK, the women's shelter said that you would offer a reduced fee or deferred payment."

"That's right Mary. Don't worry about the money right now. When we get to the point where the property has been settled, we will see where we are and discuss payment. The fee will also be reduced. My wife and I do

one or two cases like this for the women's shelter a year.
It is our way of giving back."

"Well, thank you (she screamed in her mind). You are a
God send."

"I will call again when I get the motion from his attorney.
You take care of your self in the meantime."

After hanging up the phone, she rolled down the window.
The cold wind hit her face and helped her from slipping
into a panic. She knew that she needed a clear head to
navigate the rush hour toll way traffic. Breathing deeply,
she quelled the rising fear to stop the panic.

Popping a tape into the tape player, she sang herself
home.

Piggies

She checked her makeup before adjusting the rear view mirror and settling in the driver's seat for a long, ugly phone call with her divorce attorney.

"What I don't understand is this. Why is he allowed to file for sole custody and create this financial burden? Shouldn't he have some basis for a custody petition? I am a great mom. I stayed home and cared for my children for twelve years instead of pursuing a career. When I did go back, it was part time."

"I have given you letters from the pediatrician, dentist and school telling you that I have been the parent involved in making sure the children get the care they need. Each of these letters tells you that my children have received the best level of care through me."

"How can a man file for sole custody without SOME kind of foundation? All of my activities revolve around the children. They are not left alone so that I can pursue self interests. I have never been unfaithful. I don't go out except with the children or if he is home to care for them. When I do go out it is for some school or community related function that can include the children if they so choose."

"I have also given you letters from people in the community who are in child related professions. The school superintendent, the township youth director, among others have vouched for my parenting and contributions to the community."

My oldest son's second grade teacher came up to me at the school yesterday, threw her arms around me and began to cry. She was extremely upset after hearing the gossip that my husband was trying to take my children away from me. This is not something that I am telling people so it must be coming from him. She told me' "he was never there for them, you were always there, for everything at school."

"Desperation sank in when I realized that she would not be so upset if she did not think that it was possible. She thinks he has a chance of taking my kids away, even though I have been devoted to them for the past thirteen years and am considered a great parent in my community! So tell me, WHY WOULD SHE THINK THAT? Does this happen? She must have seen it before! Tell me what I am up against for God's sake!"

"OK, calm down. Let me talk for awhile. I told you that I would be honest with you and I am going to be. But whatever the situation, I need you to remain calm and strong. Falling apart will not help you under any circumstances." Her attorney paused and cleared his throat after Mary whispered, "OK."

"The fact that your husband has filed for sole custody means that he wants a battle. It does not mean that he will be able to take your children away. To do that, he will need to prove that you are an incompetent mother. And unless you fly off the handle and give him some evidence of that, it won't happen. However, the way that the system works is either parent can petition for custody. Without an agreement by the parents on custody, the court will order psychological evaluations of the family, conciliation and mediation sessions, they may even appoint the children an attorney of their own. It can become expensive and take a long time. It all depends on how much your husband wants to fight. And judging by my conversation with him, I can tell you that he is hell bent on fighting. So I need you to settle down for a long, drawn out process. As long as he will not agree to joint custody, the court will do everything it can to get you to agree, including all kinds of mediators, counselors and all of that."

"In the end, if you still can't agree, there will be a custody hearing. These hearings can last several days and costs tens of thousands of dollars in court costs and attorney's fees. But unless you want to give up your parental rights, this is the only course we have."

"It may be that this is what your friend has experienced. She may have seen her students mothers give up the fight and relinquish their parental rights. Women are at a financial disadvantage, especially if, as in your case, they have been homemakers and do not have an independent income."

"In your experience, what was the longest case in the county," Mary asked impulsively.

The attorney took a deep breath and after a soft groan said, "seven years."

"Christ, how can that be allowed? What the hell kind of system is this?"

"It is a system that wants people to agree."

"Well, you've talked to my soon to be X. What do you think are the chances of that?"

"He sounds like a man out for revenge. He sounds irrational and full of rage. That is not good. It usually means that the case will take a long time. And it means that you need to take precautions for your safety. Don't be afraid to call me in a crisis. But please begin to find ways to keep yourself safe. Continue to talk to the women's shelter. Have plans for escape and have several safe harbors set up for you and the kids just in case. I can't stress this enough."

Mary felt herself quieting. She needed to be clear.

"With all of the focus on domestic violence and children's rights, how can this be the process? How can this be our only course?"

"The focus brings attention to the problems. It doesn't mean they have been solved. Quite honestly, this is a bad time in the system for someone in your situation. The protection just is not there. The courts focus on the laws and the system isn't equipped to handle the rest. But you have me. I will help you through this. And you need to find others that can support you through this. Because it looks like you will need a lot of support. And it looks like this will take quiet awhile."

"Thanks. Thanks for taking the time to help me understand this. And thanks for your honesty. I need it."

"Take care Mary."

The conversation ended just as Mary pulled into the parking lot. A quick check of her watch showed her that she was late for her meeting. But she could not lift her head of the car seat head rest. She needed a moment to digest the conversation. *Piggies*, by the Beatles came on the radio. She closed her eyes and lost herself in the song until it ended.

Just another attorney on the case

Listening to the children's attorney, she felt his office begin to whirl around her. Her eyes opened wider and wider as she slowly sat back in the chair and slumped down. Letting all of the air out of her lungs unintentionally, there was a pause before she could bring the air back in. She had to will it. It would not come on its own. She gave it everything she had as time took vertical flight and she lost her bearings. Just breathe.

"Does this surprise you?" the newly court appointed children's guardian asked. He seemed a little annoyed. At her last court date in family court, the judge had appointed an attorney for the children because of all the conflict surrounding them. It occurred to her that this man believed that she wanted nothing to do with her children, that she had never been a real mother to them. And that, as her soon to be X husband told this man, she was planning to walk out the door and never look back. Planning to leave him and the children.

"I don't know what you have heard about me, but let me explain to you my position in this case. Maybe then you will understand." It never occurred to her that she would not be believed until now. The world was beginning to see her as a person that she did not resemble. That invisible part of her that moved through her physical body and created the spirit, expressed the soul. It seemed to be turning into something strange without any effort from her. People were turning who she was into a monster, someone that she would never approach or appreciate. How is this happening? So out of control. Would she remember who she really was when it was all over? Would she even be the same person when they were finished ripping her to shreds?

Composing herself, straightening herself in the chair, she looked directly at the children's attorney and began to explain herself. Her choices. Her relationships with her children. Her relationships with the world. She gave him references so that he could do some research. School contacts, the pediatrician's and dentist's numbers, her employer. She challenged him to find the truth for himself. But wondered if he would take the time. Was he just another player in the courtroom scene who cared very little and did only what was necessary to move this case off his desk for the day. Usually postponing it for another day. While day after day, home remained a terrifying place for her and her children.

Wrapping up the interview, the attorney asked, "is there anything that I can do on behalf of the children right now?"

"Yes, you can ask the court to create a schedule giving me and their dad equal time to be with the children."

"Well, usually that is done at the time of the actual divorce. What is happening now, when do you spend time with your children?"

"Now, I am not allowed to spend time with my children. If I talk to them, he starts yelling at me to get away from them. If I try to take them somewhere, he blocks the doorway and won't let them leave. If I try to cook for them, he comes into the kitchen , screams at us and throws the food in the garbage." She stopped there, knowing there was more she could say, but hoping that was enough.

He looked as if he did not believe her. He asked, "What do you propose?"

"I suggest that you enter a court order designating every other day of the week for one of us. Then at least I will be able to take the children somewhere without interference. We can have meals together away from the conflict."

His eyes did not move away from her for a moment. There was a long silence which she did not feel compelled to break. She allowed him to continue to examine her face, her eyes, her determination and her honesty. "Consider it done," he said. She rose quickly from her chair and extended her hand to him, looking now at him in disbelief. She walked out into the bright sunlight to her car. The air was warm and stifling.

She sat back in the drivers seat and tried to remember who she was. She wondered if anyone knew her anymore. She was sure that no one cared. Or if they did, it was in their own comfortable way. A way that did not require them to see her pain, to understand the chaos in her life. People would ask how she was, if there was anything they could do…how many would turn away if they knew the truth. Many. She looked at her hand and guessed there were more fingers than friends who would not turn away. But she may have some.

It looked like she would at least have to ask for help. Ask to find out who would turn away and who would stay. It would just mean more loss. She would lose some people in her life because she would know who is not willing to step into her nightmare and help get her through. She could tell herself that she was better off without them. But what if "they" were everyone? What if she was asking too much? What if everyone was just as afraid and unable to do anything to stop the nightmare?

Someone would need to become witness to her character and integrity. But she began to wonder if anyone believed in her anymore, if anyone saw her as she saw herself.

Panic set in as she pulled the car from the curb and drove home. She began to say the Lord's Prayer to clear her mind. She said it all the way home and then poured herself into bed. She was asleep before the covers were over her.

Don't do that to me

She sat motionless in the reclining chair next to the phone. Outside she could hear the laughter and conversation of Suzanne's party. She and the children had been living in Suzanne's home since Bob was arrested yesterday for pushing her out the bedroom. She knew that he would be looking for her so she parked her car in Suzanne's garage so that he couldn't come and take it away. She did not know what was going to happen next. She did know that she did not feel like joining in a party. There was really no way for Suzanne to cancel the night before and she welcomed the safe harbor.

He had been calling all around to her friends and family to find her. She suspected that he was giving out Suzanne's number because her sister in law Pat and brother Bill had called Suzanne's and left messages for her. She knew that she had to return at least one call from her family, but she didn't know what he would do once he knew where she and the children were. The children loved being here. Suzanne's son Tom had been C. Jay's best friend since they were toddlers. But she was not sure how long they would be willing to stay. All of this spun in her head with no direction and no conclusion. With a heavy sigh, she picked up the phone.

"Hi Pat, it's Mary."

"Oh thank God. The world has been looking for you. Bob has called here at least twenty times. He thinks the children are in danger because you are, well, going crazy. What the hell is going on?"

"I assume that he gave you this number, probably to find out where I am. What do you think about what he has been saying?"

"Mary, honestly, we don't know what to think. We are very concerned about you and the children. Please tell me what is going on."

"Bob was arrested yesterday for grabbing me and pushing me out of the bedroom. Screaming, pushing, throwing, belittling, even an occasional slap have all been going on for sometime. It is escalating and I needed to draw a line. His view is that I am the crazy one and doing this to him because I want a divorce. He admits nothing and tells people I am crazy to minimize my support. Has he told you that I plan to leave him AND the children?"

"Yes, he says he will get sole custody and you will be paying him child support."

"And you believe him?"

"Mary I told you, we don't know what to believe. He keeps calling here. Now he wants to bring the children for a visit. I am so worried about the children."

"So am I."

"Why don't you just take the kids and get out of the house?"

"Apparently it is not that simple. He has filed for Sole Custody. My attorney tells me that if I take the children and leave, he could file a motion to get the children back into the only home they have ever known and would succeed. Then he could stall the divorce so long that because the children had been living with him, he may be awarded sole custody. In the mean time, he does everything he can to get me to leave because he knows this."

"I am sorry, I just can't believe that is your only option."

"Well, if you discover another one, please let me know. In the meantime, I have to ask you to stop allowing him to come over. I can't explain this, I don't know why, but every time he goes to your house without me, he comes home and is terribly abusive. I can't explain it. I have stopped counseling because my counselor, who was also our marital counselor has withdrawn his offer to testify for me. Apparently, Bob had threatened to sue so he would now be a hostile witness. I don't have anyone to help me figure this out and I don't care. All I know is, home is horrible for me and the children because he is so abusive. I know he is doing all of this to get me to leave. He wants to take the children away from me. I have no intention of leaving the children. He has been putting a lot of pressure on MY family and his to convince them that I am crazy and should just disappear."

Silence. Pat had no reaction but at least she was listening.

"The thing is Pat, I would expect his family to believe him, but why mine? Why am I not getting support from my family in this?"

"Mary, I told you that we don't know what to believe and we don't want to be involved. This is tearing me apart. I can't take it."

"Then you will tell him not to come over?"

"I don't have a problem with him coming over, I love to see the children."

"You're not listening to me. Listen carefully. Have you noticed that I am not with him when he comes over? Why do you think that is? I am telling you that when he comes home from your house, he is terribly abusive to me and the children see it. It happens every time. He is working hard to isolate me from anyone who may provide me support. I thought that you of all people would understand this."

"Well he tells me you're crazy. You tell me he is crazy. I just don't want any part of it."

"Do I have to wind up in the hospital or worse before my family is willing to understand this? I was there for you and Shawn when you needed me. Why is my family not supporting me in this crisis?"

"Don't do that to me Mary. Don't lay that on me. It is not my fault if he is hurting you."

"IF he is hurting me? IF? I am not saying it is your fault. I am asking you not to have him over. You are my family. Why is that so much to ask? I will also ask you not to tell him where I am or that you have talked to me. The last thing I need is for him to storm over here and demand the children. He has a court order to keep him away for 36 hours. If he intends to honor that, why is he so hell bent on finding us?"

"Mary, I am sorry, I can't help you. I need to think about what you have said. I can not be put in the middle of this."

"OK, Pat. You think about it," she whispered. With that she hung up the phone. The room was getting darker by the minute. Her heart sank with the sun, leaving her alone with her tears. The light and the laughter of the party went on outside without her.

I am in a dark room. There is a strange man in the room with me. I can see us both clearly, even though it is dark, as if a light shines from us instead of on us, making colors crisp and intense.

As I speak, my words take shape and float away. He grabs them and twists them sometimes breaking them into pieces.

I turn away from him and cry, "He uses my pain against me. Stop him." I know the pain is deep, running through my entire life, and he knows every inch of it. It leaves me with a feeling of helplessness and worthlessness and I fall to my knees.

I hear a door shut. Relief floods the room along with sunlight. But when the darkness leaves it takes my ability to speak. I am left without words. In the room of light, alone, I realize that I may never have the strength to speak or stand again. So I lay down. A small, blue bird appears in the room, circles around once or twice, then disappears through the ceiling.

Sorry I have not been in touch but my life has turned upside down since filing for divorce. All of the "unseen control" is completely out in the daylight now and blasting at volume ten. It is all I can do to hold myself and the children together.

I have made a couple attempts at getting an order of protection and all have failed. I filed for one after he was arrested for pushing me, but his attorney convinced holiday court to transfer it to family court because we have the divorce case there. Because the request for protection was filed as an emergency, once it got to family court, the judge declared that it was no longer an emergency since the incident occurred over 24 hours ago.

When he began throwing my things out the door and my food in the garbage as I was eating it, my attorney filed another request for an order of protection in family court. I took the kids and stayed with friends for the past few days, hoping that he would be served his court papers and calmed down by the time we got back.

When the process server failed to serve him because he could not be located, I (and a body guard) went to the house to try to talk to him. He screamed at me from the time I entered the house until the time I left. Nothing settled.

The children were crying because they wanted to go home. Even though home is a living hell, it seems to be better than staying with friends away from what is theirs.

My attorney also advised me to return home with the children before the soon to be ex filed a motion to get them back home and keep me out. I can't believe that this is happening to me. His $250/hr fancy pants attorney is very slick. So back into hell we must go. It is amazing that no one seems to care or is able to do anything about all the children are forced to witness: the abuse; the harassment; the screaming; the pushing; the swearing; the belittling; the destruction of the house as we live in it. I can't imagine what it is all doing to them emotionally.

The children volunteered to help the teenagers at the Township run their Haunted Trail behind the school tonight so I told them that I would take them home after that. Before we went, I had a long conversation with the Women's Shelter about my options and ways to protect myself. I shook from cold and terror during the whole conversation. As the time to return home approached, everything became more surreal. Taking the Haunted Trail home became poetic irony. It all seemed eerily symbolic. I felt like I was sleeping awake.

The children had an excellent time in spite of it all. They each had a role screaming and scaring the heck out of everyone. Toby posed as a tour guide and when he led his group over a bridge at the beginning of the trail, my friend Captain Jim (Commander of the local Marine Reserve Unit,) who was dressed like a troll, jumped up from under the bridge, grabbed Toby and pulled him under.

Toby's screams shook my very bones as I stood by the fire taking dollars from those about to be terrorized. He certainly perfected his scream. But his screams were always transformed into hysterical laughter eventually. Needless to say he was voiceless by the end of the night. C. Jay and his friend Tom did lots of different things on the trail to scare people. I think they had the most fun making it up as they went along. I'm sure they will talk about this for the rest of their lives.

And then the real scare. As we sat in the cold darkness, gathering our strength to go into the house, Cody whispered, "Mom, C. Jay and I will run in first and lead the way." Still playing the soldier leading the troops over the bridge.

We were all terrified, but did not want to be separated or homeless. As expected, he was at the door as we walked up. He stepped aside to let the children in and then blocked my way into the house with his body. "Why don't you just go, you don't belong here anymore. You are divorcing us." What an ass.

I finally took a deep breath and said "I am only divorcing you," as I firmly pushed against his body and ran into C. Jay's room where the boys were. We huddled in the bottom bunk like it was a fort and talked for a long time about the Haunted Trail. I was glad that they were able to scream their voices out before re-entering our own private horror. Who ever felt the bravest, Toby or C. Jay (certainly not me) would run into the kitchen for water or snacks when we needed them. I felt like I was back at a grade school sleep over. And I wondered, if I had not filed for divorce, had we not been so pulled together by his rage, would we have shared this night in this way? My hope is, that the divorce will continue to pull us together and not drive us apart.

I wish I had better news for you. I miss you so. Write soon.

mmb

Not guilty

She sat, stunned, looking at the motionless figures of three State's Attorneys seated in the row in front of her. Frozen in time, they all struggled to regain their senses.

She closed her eyes and fell into the darkness. She replayed the judge's verdict in her mind in an effort to find reason in it: " I will not allow this hearing to proceed, and not for the reasons we discussed in my chambers. There is no doubt in my mind that the events that the plaintiff claims to have happened, did happen. I believe her when she says that the defendant grabbed her by the arm and pushed her across the room. I know that his yelling and physical force must have been disturbing. But while I find this behavior onerous and despicable, because it happened in the marital bedroom, I do not find it to be criminal. I therefore find defendant not guilty of battery."

She opened her eyes and stared at the back of three heads as the events of the trial whirled in her head. One of the State's Attorneys turned around and looked carefully at the expression on her face. He asked, "are you alright?" She did not know how to reply. He asked, "what do you think?" She answered quietly, "I'm stunned."

His female partner let out a cross between a snicker and a sneer. All four left the room in silence.

As she walked slowly down the hallway of the courthouse, Toby came running up and jumped into her arms, embracing her tightly. "I love you mom," he said through his tears. Suddenly it occurred to her that this was the way the judge found to prevent Toby from having to testify.

It was ironic that she dropped previous charges herself because Bob threatened to have Toby testify against her. Knowing that Bob could convince the child to say anything, she dropped the charges hoping to spare him the trauma. But that had happened too many times. Now, Toby had an attorney and a counselor to help him through. She had to follow through with the hearing to try to stop the violence. But it didn't work really. The judge fell for the ploy this time.

She hugged Toby back with all of her love. "I love you too baby. I will see you at home." She let Toby down and he walked with shoulders sagging to his father to leave the courthouse. The State's Attorney approached her and in a soothing tone said, "You a have a fine boy there Mary." She closed her eyes and tried to smile, but silently screamed.

"Thank you," she said breathlessly and turned to walk away.

March, don't stop

"Would you please call my son from his second grade classroom? He has a doctor's appointment."

She sat in a chair near the window in the school office to wait. Toby was scheduled for his third appointment with a counselor. The counseling agency also sent someone to observe him in the classroom. Mindlessly watching out the window, she flashed back on Toby's Christmas party and the events that led her to seek counseling for him.

She was sitting on the floor talking to Toby and his friend when several other children joined in. She assumed they were all just looking for attention. Turning toward a gentle pat on her shoulder, she saw a beautiful little girl holding out her hands. There were several broken pencils in them.

"Toby broke these," she whispered. As she looked into the little girls eyes the girl said, "Why does he do that?"

A few children quickly left the group and Toby shifted uncomfortably and drew closer to her. "Toby is upset because his dad and I are divorcing. Breaking things seems to help him feel better. He breaks things because he is very upset."

She felt Toby give her a hug and leave his hand on her shoulder. The other children rejoined the group and held out things to show her too. Pieces of crayons, an action figure and a ruler were among the devastation. She let out a big sigh and reached out to receive all that was being offered.

"Thank you all so much. I am glad to see that Toby has so many friends that care about him. Divorce is so hard, but we will make it through with good friends like you. Come on now, group hug."

The children giggled and squealed while the group hug toppled to the ground. She could feel the classroom teacher watching nervously. When all but Toby had left the circle he asked, "Why did they tell you that stuff mom?"

"They told me because they care about you. Because they care, they saved that stuff for the right time when they thought they could help you. They did exactly the right thing. You are lucky to have so many great friends. Why don't you go join their game now and have fun at your party?"

Toby ran over to where the teacher was beginning to organize a game. Mary quietly left the room and burst into tears outside in the hallway.

Mary's pounding heart jolted her from her memory. Bob's truck was pulling into the parking lot. He had spotted her in the window. She braced herself for what was to come as she went outside to avoid a scene inside.

"You will not be taking Toby to the counselor anymore," he screamed as he approached her. He came within inches of her face and continued to scream words her anxiety would not allow her to hear.

Once the yelling stopped, she loudly, emphatically stated "Bob, the school has been given a copy of the court order preventing you from interfering with counseling. If I need to get a policeman to escort me to my car with

Toby, I will request we be allowed to wait in the principal's office for the officer. The choice is yours. If you are not gone by the time Toby is ready to go, this is what we will do."

She turned quickly and went back into the school. She expected him to follow, but was completely relieved when he didn't. He went back to his truck and pulled up to the curb to wait.

As she watched, the office clerk, who had apparently heard the ruckus outside asked, "Need some help Mayr?"

Mary smiled at her nickname being used. The familiarity felt comforting. "Well, he didn't follow me in. I guess you can watch to make sure Toby and I get to my car safely and call the police if there is a problem."

"We sure will. In the mean time, I will call school security over for some preliminary help."

Mary lost track of everything around her as she willed her body out of it's current panic. Slow down heart beat. Cool down body (taking off her sweater.) Toby woke her up by grabbing her arm. Looking down, she could see his concern at the sight of his father.

She bent down to help him with his coat. "It's OK baby. We are just going to march right to my car and get in. Don't stop and don't pay attention to the yelling." They both knew there would be yelling.

Toby grabbed her hand with both of his and they left the office. There was yelling, a lot of it. Bob tried to block their way off the sidewalk and they pushed past him and ran to the car. She fumbled with the key a minute as she protected Toby with her body between him and his father. Once the door opened, Toby scrambled in and Mary after him. She locked the car quickly and started it. As she tried to drive away, Bob walked in front of the car several times. She had to avoid him by backing up or swerving. But they finally made it out of the parking lot.

She was shocked to see that he did not follow them. Unbelievable.

Toby laid down and put his head on her lap. She stroked his hair slowly until her fell asleep. She felt cold and thirsty and out of breath. But relieved to be rid of him for now. She leaned back in the car seat and turned up the music to drown out the scream of shame and terror in her head.

As she sang along with Michael Bolton's *A Time for Letting Go*, she glanced down at her son. Peace was restored in his face as he lay sleeping. She marveled at a child's ability to accept the comfort of the moment so completely, and leave the rest behind.

I am on the Naval Base. I have enlisted in the Marine Corps and struggle with the job my commander has given me. I am chopping wood and the job never ends. My arms hurt terribly with every stroke of the ax. The pile of wood to be split never gets smaller. I chop faster and faster, but the workload remains the same.

I put the ax down to take a break because I can no longer lift my aching arms. I go into one of the buildings on base to look for a bathroom. I want to wash my face and cool off. After putting water on my face I look up in the mirror at my reflection. Tears come to my eyes because I know that I have a job that I can never finish.

I suddenly feel the need to run. Running out of the building I run to the lake shore. I run up the beach and realize my shoes are filling with sand and making it hard to run. I stop to take off my shoes and throw them into the lake. I continue to run and run and run.

Dear Viv,

I should be cleaning or bathing or shuffling papers or generating papers but couldn't bring myself to do any of that before I wrote to you. I suppose I simply had the urge to make it all real first. Talking to you in some form still does that to me. Why?

Things are good, relationships are good, and directions are good. Yet I find myself in an uncomfortable place of self awareness where I am not sure exactly what it is that needs to be changed, but know that the results of the change will be wonderful.

I think I am still working my way through some post traumatic stress (like Toby) and need to begin to perceive things differently. Very difficult. I have come to realize that not everyone acts consciously. Many people go from day to day reacting based on emotional scripts and somehow manage to get by just enough to keep living. The rest of us are left with finding a way to perceive and respond effectively in spite of the chaos this creates. Some want to understand, many do not.

My friend made me a Christmas card: The most visible creators I know are those artists whose medium is life itself. The ones who express the inexpressible, without brush, hammer, clay or guitar. They neither paint nor sculpt - their medium is being. Whatever their presence touches has increased life. They see and don't have time to draw. They are the artists of being alive.

I read this from time to time and it keeps me going.

Anyway, I am really struggling when presented with aggressive resistance (or passive aggressive.) Why does aggression seem to send me into an emotional reaction and how do I get myself out of this pattern? It is a scream button. And I can't seem to find the immediate objectivity needed for a response at the moment. But instead of getting myself into trouble (usually) I tend to suspend all reactions until I can formulate a response and come back. I would rather have a response without all the emotion spontaneously. Emotion and anxiety get in the way. And I am not as effective as I should be.

I had a dream that I was facing an outside wall and trying to fly. But I just couldn't get my feet off the ground. The harder I tried, the harder it became. Then a woman's voice behind me whispered "Your anxiety holds you." I relaxed and felt the anxiety without analyzing or defining it. Then I let go of it. The more the anxiety left me, the farther I flew. The air was fresh and sweet, the sky warm and blue. I just can't keep the wall away.

How is your family? I think of you often.

Love,

mmb

Headphone heaven

Bob kept inching toward her, yelling louder, his face getting redder. She couldn't even hear what he was yelling about anymore it was so overwhelming. Nothing and everything. Nothing of consequence, everything that bothered him about her. He blocked the hallway exit so that she could not leave without pushing past him.

She turned around to consider her options and saw C. Jay in his bedroom pick up his headphones, put them on, and sit down at his desk like he was in a world all his own, nothing to bother him. What a genius!

Quickly, she ducked into the bathroom and locked the door. Bob stood outside yelling for a little while until she turned on the shower. His voice faded with the soothing water. She turned on the massager and let it work on her neck and shoulders awhile.

When she finished, she opened the bathroom door and Toby was standing there.

"Hi Toby, do you want to go to Circuit City with me to look at disc players?"

"Yeah, can I get a CD?"

She heard her soon to be ex-husband his bedroom begin yelling again, "He will not be going with you"...blah blah blah.

Toby flew into his bedroom and shut the door. Mary grabbed her purse and ran out the front door. She began to shiver, but didn't know if it was from the cold autumn wind or the horrifying scenes at home. Closing and locking her car door, she rested a minute in the silence. As she pulled out of the driveway, she could see Toby looking out of his bedroom window. He waved slowly as she drove by. She picked up her cell phone and called the house. Thank goodness Toby answered. She got his CD order from him and a suggestion for one for his brother.

"Thanks mom," washed over her body like a wave of relief. She hated leaving him there. But they both knew it was the only way to stop the violence for now.

When she got home, she ran into C. Jay's room and closed the door. Whew, she made it without a confrontation. C. Jay was still at his desk with his headphones but saw her come in and came over to the bed. As she gave him his new CD, Toby came in and jumped on the bed. After handing him his prize for bravery, she pulled out her new

disc-man and headphone set.

She heard C. Jay chuckle. Their eyes met in complete understanding. "Now we can all put on our headphones when the yelling starts. Thanks, C. Jay, you are a genius!"

Toby ran and got his disc-man. They all laid on the bed, all over each other in places because the bunk bed was so small. Mary thought it was perfect. A dark, cozy little fort where they could cuddle and escape the terrors of the world. In darkness, she took the arm of Eric Clapton's *Little Wing*, "*And if she winds up walkin' the streets, loving every other man she meets, who'll be the one to answer why? Lord I hope it's not me.*" They all fell asleep fully dressed, listening to their music.

Tearing his room apart

"Toby, Toby stop!"

She could feel her youngest son begin to spiral out of control.

"No, I hate you." She wrapped her arms around him and tried the firm hug technique. Focusing on his baby picture on the wall behind him, she enveloped him in her arms and tried to hold him lovingly without force. Speaking softly into his ear, she did her best to calm him, "It's OK. It's going to be OK. Let's take a walk to the beach for a swim. We'll stop and see who can come out to play along the way."

He burst from her arms and fell into the wall behind him. His baby picture came crashing down. Nothing broken thank goodness. But this scared Toby and he ran into his bedroom and began throwing things against the wall.

She knew there was no stopping him now. He needed to continue until he was exhausted. By that time, his room was usually a shambles with a few new dents in the wall and several childhood toys broken. The counselor had advised her to let him go when he was like this. According to the counselor, Mary was to suggest that she understood his need to destroy his room like this. Little by little, she was to introduce boundaries for his rage. She wondered if this would be possible. Something like: "You can throw things around in your room, but try not to hurt yourself or anyone else." Or "you can tear your room apart, but no other room in the house." My god, how had they gotten here? Would they ever be able to leave the horror behind and restore peace in their lives?

She laid down on the floor next to his closed door. Closing her eyes, she listen to his screams and obscenities. As the crashing and banging subsided, she mustered her courage for the recovery. She needed to leave her own emotional reactions behind and help her son through this. He needed to know that they were in this together. That she loves him and always will. That he is OK and they will find a way to make everything OK. She would hold him and rock him and cry with him and reassure him. She would remind him that she would always be there for him. Even though she lacked the confidence she had been advised to show him.

Would she successfully be pushed out of the children's lives by their bully father, his highly paid attorney and a system that ignored the nightmare of her home life? She did not know. Would everything be OK, or would her children be permanently changed, emotionally crippled from the horror? She did not know. Did she have the strength to get through the next moment, day or year? She doubted it.

When all was quiet beyond the door, she slowly opened it. The room was dark and Toby was slumped over in a chair by his desk. She slowly entered the room. When he did not protest, she scooped him up in her arms and sat down on his bed with him in her lap. She sang his favorite lullaby while they rocked. She kissed his cheek, stroked his hair and softly sang *Love is Real*. He nestled right into her, accepting all of the comfort she had to offer.

Missing Music

She stared hard into the empty cupboard. She sat, surrounded by the contents of the hutch, her mother's hutch, that he had emptied all over the floor. She wondered what had been taken, what was left. Her spinning mind could not remember what was kept in the hutch. Photos, old keepsakes, pieces of the children's infancy, pieces of the marriage, some were gone, some left. She wondered if she would ever miss any of it, whatever it was.

The she remembered her albums. Gone. She had painstakingly collected all of the record albums that were stolen from her in college. Searched second had music stores to recapture the music that brought comfort inside. Steve Winwood's double album; Argent; Soft Machine; Laura Nyro – gone, all gone. Stolen again. Why? The turntable was still connected to the stereo. They would become trash somewhere, all of the songs that meant so much, that were still *playing in her spirit.*

Thank God he was gone. Now she could begin to pick up the pieces, the contents of the hutch and everything else left in the wake of a destructive marriage. But she wondered if she would ever hear that treasured music again.

Letting go – she decided then not to begin again to search music stores to try to recapture the collection. This will just have to be a part of letting go. She wondered if she would be letting go of the music, the past, a part of her spirit she just couldn't hold on to. That was ripped from her like the dream of a happy family.

As she walked around the house, every room was the same, drawers emptied on the floors, closet contents thrown all over. Why? Heading downstairs she heard herself gasp half way down. Slowly, she sat down on the step. The basement was flooded because the hot water heater had been removed. The furnace had been taken apart and the central air, air cleaner, duct work removed. And, of course, all of the "stuff" in the basement had been thrown about. Head in hands, she sobbed.

When the tears ran out, she rose and walked outside. The cool breeze on her face felt good. As she opened her eyes and walked around back of the house, the empty yard and trampled flower beds stopped her. Everything was gone: lawn furniture, AC unit, and children's play equipment. With a heavy sigh she turned and noticed the side door of the garage open slightly. As she walked in she began to laugh at the unsettling contrast of complete order within the garage. Everything was as neat as a pin and a small office had been set up. Of course! The judge had ordered Bob to remove only his personal belongings and vacate the house, but gave him an additional 30 days to remove his company's equipment from the garage. Well, this was a statement. He was still here and not leaving.

After the final divorce hearing, Bob had refused to leave the house as agreed. He continued to storm, telling the children that their mother would be leaving, not him. She had to go back to court and have him court ordered out of the home, even though the divorce agreement had already done so. It looked like he would be keeping a daily vigil in the garage.

Startled out of her deep thought, she noticed a telephone on the desk. There had not been a phone in the garage before! She followed the wire out of the garage, over the sidewalk and into a hole drilled through the house into the basement. Shaking her head, she removed the phone, took it inside and locked the house up tight.

The children were not expected home until 8:30. She called her attorney and left a message describing her home and suggesting they file for change in custody. Joint custody would never work. This was insanity. The mediator appointed at the time of the divorce resigned after two sessions. Now this.

She decided to walk down to the beach and think this through. With the weather turning cold, she would need to act quickly. Each step she took weighed down her heart. By the time she reached the lake she was sure that she could cry enough tears to flood the banks. She sat on the pier and dangled her feet in the water. She could not bear to look at her reflection so she kept the water moving. Where were her children? What were they thinking? What permanent wounds would this put in their hearts, in their spirits. How would they all survive this?

She lay back on the pier and closed her eyes. She fell asleep as the sunset continuously changed her color. She woke to twilight and the sound of children playing. Walking home, she braced herself for the next trauma.

Rounding the corner she could see his car in the driveway. Her stomach turned as if it had just wretched. As she walked to the house she could hear him yelling at the children. Within eyesight, she could see that he was lifting one of them to the kitchen window, trying to get them in.

"Haven't you taken everything you need, or is there something in that mess you forgot?"

He began to scream something about the phone and she blocked it out. She went to the door and unlocked it.

Standing in the doorway, she allowed the children to run past her and stood her ground, preventing any one else from entering.

When the yelling had stopped, she said "You and your friends are no longer welcome in the house. The house will be locked when I am not home. I will not allow my phone service to be used in the garage." The yelling started again. Turning a deaf ear, she closed the door and bolted it. She rested her head on the door she whispered to herself, "the children." Turning around, she noticed the message indicator light on the phone blinking. With a heavy sigh, she went to check on the children.

Hi Vivi,

I hope this letter finds you well and happy. And I hope my last phone call didn't cause any problems...my dreams often have more to do with me than anyone else. But I needed to be sure of you, that you didn't need me and you were OK. I would like to see you somehow. Come out here. My life is settling down - emotionally anyhow. I am doing more traveling for business. My ability to reach my goals has grown considerably since distancing myself from Bob and limiting his ability to sabotage. I applied for a mortgage to build a town house and will be buying a new car next month. Finances were difficult at first with no child support or maintenance. But it turned out to be very nice not having to depend on anyone for anything. Making my decisions independently and creating my own reality feels wonderful.

I'm doing very well professionally and feel good about that. But more than that I feel as if everything is coming together for me, and that I have begun a spiritual flight of some kind. I am again free to explore people, places, relationships, meta-realities and realities at my own pace according to my own need. I am learning a tremendous amount on every level and feel great about that. Life is difficult, but good. I think it's because of where I am that I find myself thinking of you so often. We began many journeys together, discovered many of life's aspects together. I think that adolescence and midlife have much in common. They both require intensive self examination and re-creation. Don't you think it would be a good time for us to find each other again? We could compare these two important life phases together. We could provide history for each other. We always did have a unique way of providing perspective for each other, like water to a thirsty child.

Anyway, I feel like I have done a good job of the work required in midlife. Just as in adolescence, I have watched many people get lost here. But I have a lot yet to do, and look forward to it with joy and enthusiasm.

My boys are doing well. We are staying close to work out all the remaining anger and difficult emotion remaining from the divorce. As long as we continue to work, I know we will make it. These boys are both extraordinary people. Each very different. I know that you will love them both.

I still have not seen much of my family since divorce proceedings began over two years ago. Bob used them against me very badly. Fear and confusion keep them away. But if I don't forgive my family, I couldn't forgive myself I suppose. We all come from the same place. I hope we manage to find each other again when this is all over.

Please take a couple of minutes and rip something off to me. Don't worry about saying anything meaningful or coherent. I obviously don't. A wave of joy always hits me when I read words put together as only you can do it.

Love, mmb

Can't do this anymore

As she sat in the chair outside the courtroom, she realized that she could not feel the chair. She could only feel the tears streaming down her face as she tried with all her might to control her breathing and not break into a sob.

"I'm finished. I can't do this anymore," she said between breaths.

"Oh now, what does that mean?" said her attorney sitting next to her. He sounded annoyed. His annoyance startled her for a moment. Then she realized that he thought she meant life, she cannot continue to live. Maybe she did mean that.

She paused and took a long, measured breath before speaking. "I meant that I am finished in the courtroom. The judge made it clear that the courts do not care about the abuse and harassment. They are not willing to do anything about it. No one cares. No warning, no reprimand, no judgment. If this judge sincerely thinks that I am strong enough to continue to live like this, he is dead wrong. I am watching my children deteriorate too. He heard the testimony about Toby's violent outbursts and problems with counseling. No one cares. Somehow, I am going to have to protect myself and my kids and not worry about this parenting agreement. He has broken it so many times, it is not worth anything. And no one cares. What the hell did that judge mean, "I will not rule in favor of either parent because ruling in favor of the mother would cause the father to alienate the children from her. And ruling in favor of the father would not be in the children's best interest." Doesn't the court see that he is already alienating the children? He couldn't try any harder to do that. The judge just doesn't care. I guess I will just have to let go of my need to care so much for my children. Lots of parents don't care as much. Giving them things like braces and tutors and college may just not be possible. He will never agree to anything I suggest. The children will always be put in the middle and used as conflict bait. I will always be the enemy. Everyone sees what he is doing and no one cares."

It all came pouring out without prior thought. She did not know where it came from because her body was numb and her mind blank to her. Like looking into an empty mirror. She could not see herself in her mind. She could not feel herself in that chair. All she knew was the resounding phrase "no one cares." As she closed her eyes, she ripped in two. On person sat paralyzed in front of the empty mirror. The other turned to her attorney as he mustered some empty encouragement.

"This judge gave a non verdict, made no decision. It could be the basis for appeal."

Looking her attorney dead in the eye, she told him "No, I'm finished here. After three days of examination on the witness stand, being torn apart, losing friends that I have asked to testify because his attorney ripped them apart also, hearing his laughter as he left the courtroom…there is no way I would do this again." She wiped the tears from her face and stood to leave. Half of her stood to leave. The other half remained seated in front of the empty mirror.

Shielding the stare

Before she knew it, she was up on her feet, screaming loud and long. C. Jay had the ball and out ran the pack over the goal line for the first touch down of the game.

It always amazed Mary that in this instance, she reacted before she was conscious of doing so. When her son had the football, and his knees reached a certain height in his run, she knew no one could catch him. And she was on her feet, screaming, sometimes running along with him if not surrounded by a crowd. There was nothing that matched that thrill. She gave up being embarrassed about this reaction a long time ago. Nothing would stop the joy, not even the fact that she sometimes looked like an idiot cheering for her son.

As she was wrapping a blanket around her to ward off the cold, she heard "Hi Mary."

A group of friends sat down behind her. After saying hello, she noticed that she was suddenly surrounded by friends. They were parents of children in C. Jay's class that she had known for years, and had seen her through her divorce and stood by her. Her friends Suzanne and Donna were among them.

She knew from experience that being suddenly surrounded by this group could only mean one thing. Her X was staring at her, that hateful, contemptuous stare that she had become immune to long ago. It started during the divorce in the courtroom. Then, her attorney would strategically position himself to protect Mary. Soon it began happening at every available opportunity, such as when they both attended events for the children. Sometimes people would come over and mention it, and stay by her, squirming uncomfortably in their chairs and talking softly to themselves about it. Sometimes it was not even mentioned. Protection was quietly provided.

Mary leaned back and whispered to Donna, "Is he staring again?"

"Yep. I knew we were in trouble when I got within feet of him at the concession stand and the smell of booze almost bowled me over."

Because there was nothing she could do about the way he stared at her, Mary learned to ignore her X all together in public. But when suddenly surrounded like this, she knew the reason. Everyone's heart was in the right place. They were shielding her from him. More importantly, they were showing her children that they understood the danger of their father's behavior, and their support for their mother.

Although she was deeply ashamed, she was also grateful for the protection, and the message that it sent to her X. It amazed her that he was not at all deterred by the protection. She knew that at any time during this game now, she turned to look at him, she would see that contemptuous glare again.

She leaned back and put her head on Donna's knee and felt the warmth of a pat on her head. Feeling thirsty, she briefly considered getting up to get some water from the concession stand but then thought better of it. If these friends could stand the fact that she screamed like a banshee every other play when her son carried the ball, it was worth staying to bask in the comfort of the safety they came to provide.

Hope your Valentine's Day is full of love. Sounds like with all of those new George family additions there is lots of opportunity for celebration in your life now.

The boys and I managed to have a very tender Valentine's Day together. You will enjoy the sweetness that each of them has developed. They were a little squirrelly after spending an entire week with their dad, who has chose to live in a world of denial and self deception that is very sad to witness. I have managed to detach myself from it quite successfully, but helping the children understand and care for themselves while within is difficult.

Toby is still experiencing depression and post traumatic stress after the divorce. He recently had a psych eval to determine whether medication will help. I was unable to get Bob to recognize or engage in this process until the medication was prescribed and then we were in court the next day so he could stop it. The judge ordered a second opinion so here we go again.

The first thing I noticed was a print of Freud on the wall of the doctor's office. (Didn't look good for me huh?)

It was an amazing meeting. Very interesting to watch. I found myself so caught up in the process going on between Bob and the doctor I often lost my cue to respond.

Bob has created such an unreal way of seeing things to protect himself. This keeps him in a very mechanical level of perception. He seems to have lost all insight into life and himself. Very sad. All Dark. He denies Toby's depression. He denies the role that alcohol and addiction play in his life. He recites the many correct responses he has learned, and then contradicts himself when the focus of the conversation changes. But the most amazing thing to watch is his ability to psychologically manipulate. I have watched every therapist and even this doctor fall into it. But this time the doctor recognized it after his button had been pushed. He verbalized it without Bob understanding. Many long silences waiting for Bob's understanding that never came. It was difficult and sad but quite interesting.

The boys and I continue to live and grow in spite of it all. It has given me tremendous insight into human nature and relationships and care for the soul. And it has given me the opportunity to teach some difficult life lessons to the boys while they are in my care. They have managed, in spite of all the fear and pain, to hold on to their decency and ability to do their best. We continue to work on faith and consciously developing character. I see their depression as the condition of that work, and know that as long as we continue loving and talking and holding each other, we will learn what we need to live a good life together. They are both amazing people and I am quite lucky to have them for Valentines.

Construction on the town house is slow. A move by the end of April is our best estimate. The boys will be glad to have their own rooms. I will be glad to have the tax relief and extra room, but most of all the fire place. Cozy place to dream. I haven't stopped enjoying that.

I'm not quite sure how I got here, but it's a good enough place to be. I have a strong circle of friends, two excellent children and the wherewithal to live comfortably as life unfolds and carries my spirit into flight. As long as I continue to fly, I find the joy needed to endure life's difficulties.

In my dreams, I still fly with you. As always, it was wonderful to hear from you. Give my best to the family.

Much love,

mmb

I am getting the mail from the mail box. As I put the key into the box I get a huge electric shock. The shock throws me back on the grass and I sit there and cry. An old man comes by walking his old dog. They stop and the dog asks if he can help. I tell the man that I can't get my mail out of the box. He takes my key and has no trouble opening it. He hands me back the key and resumes his walk.

I reach in and get my mail. With the mail is a small box, no return address. I open the box and an eye rolls out. It lands on the grass in a dry dead spot. It rolls a little before it stops and stops with the iris up, looking at me. I realize that it is my X's eye.

I drop the rest of the mail on the eye and run home.

M&M terror

Donna's husband Jim quickly grabbed her, spilling some of the M&Ms he had just offered her, before she fell off the bleachers.

"It's OK, sit back there. Are you OK? Wow.

"I am so sorry. I don't know why I reacted like that. That was really strange. I must be tired."

"It's OK," he said again not quite knowing how to reassure her.

The conversation came to an abrupt halt after that. Jim focused on the basketball game. She saw Donna, his wife coming through the crowd to sit with them. She was glad for the distraction from the awkward situation.

As Jim and Donna began their marital chat, she wondered at her over reaction. Jim had simply offered her some of the M&Ms he was eating. The motion of his arm coming toward her in her peripheral vision startled her so violently she would have fallen from the bleachers if he hadn't grabbed her arm.

She had been jumpy lately. Lots of things had scared her. People coming around a corner unexpectedly. Or the times when the children making a sudden noise when she was deep in thought. She screamed and scared them back once. They thought that was funny.

She knew that she was much too nervous, but did not know what to do about it. She started drinking chamomile tea at night. She meditated for one half hour every morning. She walked with her dog twice a day. Well, she would have to find more ways to settle down. She resolved to search the internet for stress busting techniques.

"Hey, how ya doin'?" Donna broke her thought. Suddenly, the crowd broke into a cheer.

"Good job C. Jay," Jim yelled. Mary just caught the end of C. Jay's lay up out of the corner of her eye. She jumped up and cheered for him. A cold chill ran up her spine from the excitement. She was feeling very raw.

"Guess I better start watching the game," she said with a laugh to Donna as she sat back down.

Covered in bruises

Looking into the steel blue eyes of Toby's counselor, she moved around in her chair to find her center. She wanted to be calm and thoughtful in her response but the issue upset her on many primal levels.

"How often does Toby hit me? I can honestly say that my body is covered in bruises." She raised her shirt sleeves and pant legs to illustrate. "When he looses control, he strikes out wildly."

"What do you do then?"

"Well, if I think he can calm down, I will hold him firmly in a hug and talk to him softly until he calms down. That used to work when he was little. Sometimes it still works. When it doesn't, or if I think he is too out of control, tell him to come see me when he calms down and leave the room. At that point, he usually tears the room apart. The mess I can pick up. The holes in the walls and door and the marks on the furniture are another matter. I had even resigned myself to them, but today he picked up a knife in the kitchen, took it into the bathroom and tried to cut his arm with it. That is when I called you. He has swung knives around before, but never used it on himself or anyone else. I have run out of ways to help him."

"He has seen two psychiatrists. One recommended meds, the second recommended "family counseling" only. You are his third therapist. While my X won't participate in counseling, he finds a way to get a change in therapists as soon as the counseling threatens his control over my son."

"OK, let me talk to him awhile." The counselor looked serious and concerned.

Mary felt cold and thirsty so she walked over to the coffee machine and poured herself a cup while the counselor took Toby into her office. As she turned to sit down next to C. Jay, his dad stormed in and yelled, "C. Jay, come out here and talk to me." C. Jay looked at his mother, stood slowly and followed his father out the door.

Trying hard to contain a scream of frustration, she slumped in her chair. The door flew open again and Bob took the seat across from her yelling, "I want to know exactly what is going on here."

"Well, I asked for an emergency session because Toby was trying to cut his arm with a kitchen knife. I left a message for you because I am required to do so in the parenting agreement."

"I don't believe that. You're the only one with the problem here. Toby is just fine when he is with me. I want to talk to that counselor." With that he jumped up and headed for the counselor's office. She could hear him yelling in there. He returned remarkably quickly and sat down in a quiet, angry huff.

About thirty minutes later, the counselor came out and asked Bob to come into her office. As they walked down the hall, she turned to Mary and gave her a wink. Toby came out of the office a minute afterward. They all sat listening to the yelling.

"I want to go home," cried Toby.

"OK, I just want to make sure the counselor doesn't need to speak to me again."

"What's going to happen?" asked C. Jay.

"Well, we just have to have faith that everything will be alright."

"Why are you always talking about faith? I don't believe there is a God that will make everything alright. I just don't believe that anymore." He sounded so angry.

"Well honey, if I were you, I would probably feel the same way right now. You have been through a lot. But there are lots of different kinds of faith. Faith in God is not the only kind. Do you believe in yourself?"

"Yes," he said in a low voice, eyes cast downward.

"Do you believe that if you do your best, you can succeed."

"Yeah," he said with disgust because it was just another thing he was tired of hearing from his mother.

"Do you believe that the sun will rise tomorrow?"

He looked up in surprise and answered, "Yes."

While she had eye contact she added "Do you believe I love you?"

"Yes" he said with a smile.

"OK, that's a lot to believe in. And that's all faith is really, believing."

While she met C. Jay's smile Toby came over to her and put his arms around her.

"Mom, I will be OK. I want to go home, please."

"Well, OK. I will call the counselor and ask her to call me on my cell phone. Let's go. And Toby....thank you for working this through. It was very important. C. Jay, thanks for your help. We need to stick together as a family to get through this. If we stay together, we will get through this."

C. Jay came over and joined the hug. They all laughed softly and rose to leave.

Family Values

Arriving at the county's social services recognition dinner, Mary felt exhausted. She gave her coat to check in and took the receipt. Looking around, she hesitated to walk into the dining area. She decided to go to the ladies room first and make sure that she was presentable, even though she had done so before leaving home 10 minutes ago. It seemed difficult to leave the strain of her home life behind for a night.

Suzanne breezed toward her and squeezed her arm. "You look fabulous," she sang.

After spending far too much on the Donna Karen suit chosen for this evening, Mary decided to go all out and have her hair and nails done by the local diva stylist. When her boss notified her that she would be honored at an annual dinner for the county's who's who, she was petrified. Never having mastered the art of public speaking, she dreaded that moment of having all eyes in the room on her.

"Thanks," she muttered as she hugged her friend. "How many people are here?"

"A couple hundred I'd say," Suzanne laughed. "Relax, you'll be fine. Just pretend they are all children. After all, that's what this award is all about, your work with our children!"

"Those children do all the work. I'm just the token adult that opens the door."

"Come on Mary. Give it up. Accept the honor with a gracious thanks so you can relax and have a little fun tonight."

"Fun? Hmmm, what's that?"

Suzanne chuckled. She knew all too well what Mary had been going through lately because she had often been the person Mary turned to in tears.

"Well, if you don't know, you are about to find out. I'll make sure of that!" Suzanne cried as she steered Mary into the dining area.

Suzanne secured them a table near a fireplace with a roaring fire. Comfort zone. Excellent. Donna, Debra, Kate and Judy were already seated and smiling brilliantly for her as she approached the table.

"Take a deep breath Mary. You don't exactly look happy to be here."

"I just hope they call my name soon, so I can get over with it and relax," Mary said as she almost missed her chair trying to sit. The laughter calmed her and her friends worked to get her into shape to face the crowd.

The first part of the evening was a blur of anticipation. After a short, humble speech while accepting her award, Mary finally relaxed enough to mix and mingle. When she left her table to go to the ladies room after dinner, she did not return for more than an hour, being delayed by person after person wanting to meet her and talk about her work at the Township.

In the soft light of the ballroom, she found herself opening up to her community and the people in it. She felt wonderful, talking about her work and the children that made it all possible. She was transported for a while, from the intensity and struggle of her divorce.

Then it happened. As she was talking to a group of local experts on "Parenting" that had cornered her, Mary was boldly asked; "I hear that you are going through a difficult divorce. I know that can be very hard. How are you holding up?"

It occurred to Mary that a couple of the county's judges that heard her divorce case were in this room, along with the local State's Attorney and people from his office who worked on her case.

She felt her stomach turn and said, "Yes, it is very difficult. Will you excuse me? I am very thirsty. I think I will go to the bar for a club soda."

"I'll get that for you," said someone in the group that she did not recognize. Great, just great. No escape here!

"How do you do it? How do you cope so beautifully?"

Mary pushed aside all the implications of that question and tried to think quickly.

"Well, it has been very difficult. But I think the adversity brings my children closer together and closer to me. Strength is something that is learned with practice. And we are getting plenty of practice."

The laughter calmed her a bit. Her nameless friend returned with her club soda and she took a long drink before continuing, conscious of the fact that all eyes were on her and completely focused on what she was saying.

"I suppose the best thing to come out of this is that I have been forced to think clearly about what values I want to hand down to my children. They are getting so many mixed messages as the divorce plods on that I feel the need to reinforce the positive values that will get us through the difficulty."

"We have a clear glass cookie jar at home with "Family Blessings" painted on the lid. When something good happens to one of us, we write it on a slip of paper and put it in the jar. Part of our holiday tradition for New Year and Easter is to look at all of the blessings and talk about them. It keeps us focused on the positive and helps create our family history."

"What a great idea! Where did you get the jar? Did you paint it yourself?"

"Yes," said Mary with a blush. "It wasn't hard." She went on, feeling propelled to keep the conversation going to stop the personal questions.

"We also have another tradition for New Year's that the children enjoy. It began when they were young enough to accept it. New Year's activities are always such a challenge. It is a long time until midnight!."

Again, the laughter calmed her down.

"I created three binders, one for each of us. There are twelve pages, each with a narrative on one of our "family values" and then some pages at the end for each of us to write our goals for the coming year. We sit at the table with three candles and three gifts each

before us. We each read a page, one of us lights a candle and then we all open one of our gifts. The children weren't to keen on having to read a page of such heady stuff, especially my youngest. But they enjoy the presents and the candle lighting. I did wonder if they were understanding what they were reading until I saw some of it show up in their school work!"

"How fabulous! What are the values? What is it they are reading?"

"Well, let's see if I can remember. There are really three categories: Friendship, Family and Self Determination. The friendship category includes compassion, gratitude and fairness. The Family chapter includes respect, responsibility and unity. The Self Determination: honesty, peace and faith. Wow! I can't believe I remembered that so clearly! But there you have it. Some of the material I found in books. Some I added from my own experience. I was surprised that my children enjoyed it. They look forward to it like Christmas morning. Last year my youngest was saying, 'is it time yet?'"

"My youngest enjoys setting his goals for the year. My oldest, not so much. But after all the candles are lit and the presents are opened, we review our last years goals and set new ones. I think it is good for them to see me set my goals and achieve them. Since we started, there has been only one goal that I have not achieved. So they watched me set the same goal for next year and helped me celebrate when I finally achieved it. I think it helps me as much as it does them."

"What kind of goals do you set for yourself?"

Mary smiled at the personal nature of the question. She was now feeling anxious about the intentions of this audience.

"Last year one of my goals was to buy a town home and move us in. The town home is being built now and I will be closing by the end of the summer. I set three big goals that require life or lifestyle changes. The children set goals for their grades, or their sports, or changes that require work over time."

Before tonight, Mary had not shared this information with anyone. These holiday traditions were some of her desperate attempts to help the children understand life and what they were going through. And just maybe a way for her to understand it too. But it now occurred to her that she had not told friends or family about these traditions. And she didn't know why.

Mary let out a heavy sigh as she listened to the conversation around her and nodded politely. She then excused herself after Suzanne approached and suggested they get a drink together.

"Thanks, I don't like to talk about myself. Who knows what those people think of me? I was a little uncomfortable about the fact that they knew things about me I did not tell them."

"Well Mayr, people talk. You can't stop that. Forget them and help me remember the drink order for our table."

Standing at the bar, Mary closed her eyes and tried to slow the speed of the mixed emotions swirling within her.

Slow down Mary Margaret. You will get through this.
You will. Will you?

If I am the only person willing

Her feet were firmly planted in the middle of the courthouse hallway floor. She knew that she was blocking traffic and was glad of it. She knew that her voice was much too loud and that pleased her too, even fueled her determination. She could feel her divorce attorney's eyes on her and see him shift position over and over out of the corner of her eye. She vaguely wondered what he thought of the charge she had just begun.

"Well let me tell you something, as attorney for the children you have not been able to stop my X from interfering with Toby's counseling at every turn. Now you don't seem to care about it one way or another. Why haven't you asked what his grades are, what concerns his teachers have or what behavior changes are troubling? Why is your only question to me 'How could you take him to counseling at the Women's Shelter?'"

The children's attorney took her arm and pulled her aside, out of the way of the small crowd that was gathering around. He lowered his voice in an effort to get her to lower hers. Little did he know the level of her desperation and determination. She refused to acknowledge the brick wall the system had placed before her.

Before he could respond to her tirade, she continued without lowering her voice. "Let me tell you the answers to those questions you think so unimportant. Toby is failing every subject. Why you don't ask? Because this horrible situation created by YOUR recommendation of Joint Legal Parenting gets worse and worse and Toby is giving up on the world and himself. He doesn't respond at all when they call his name in class. I suppose that does not concern you either. Well let me tell you something, if I am the only person in this world that cares about what is happening to Toby, I can assure you that will be enough to help him. And if the local women's shelter is the only place that will counsel him without his father's interference, then THEY WILL COUNSEL HIM. And if you don't like that, and the court does not like that, they had better see to it that he gets the help he needs without the threats and intimidation from his father. Toby' father made sure that he cannot take medication that might be helpful. Toby's father has threatened to sue three counselors who then refused to treat us, even with court orders. Why is there no consequence for his violating these orders? Is that in my son's best interest? You leave us without options."

The Guardian led her by the arm to seats in the hall and gently guided her into a chair.

"Mary, lower your voice."

Mary sprung up and stood before him. "I will not!"

"I want everyone listening to know how this system chews up children and spits them out, while their parents have court date after court date without resolution. Why? Because these courts haven't a clue as to how to deal with issues of mental illness in parents and domestic violence in cases of divorce. In the mean time, my son sinks further and further into despondence and violence of his own until I am covered in bruises trying to help him and the school begs me to do something because he shut down in the classroom. And what is your solution? Schedule another court date, then another and another. Tack more money on to the endless attorney's fees that will land my family into bankruptcy. Tie my hands so that I cannot access help for my son without violating a court order. Tell me – who are your court orders protecting now. Certainly not my children, Mr. Guardian."

The guardian stood up before Mary was finished and looked away.

"Oh I see. We are done here because you say we are done. You think your embarrassment will end this? Well then, let me summarize for everyone in the hallway."

Mary was well aware that all eyes were on her. She looked directly into the eyes of the Guardian before she continued.

"I can sum it up in two words. YOU SUCK! This system SUCKS!"

She stopped to breathe. Her attorney stood across the hallway with a look of amazement on his face. The children's attorney had turned a deep shade of red and was sputtering something about speaking with Mr. X's attorney and the judge. When he left she sat in the chair nearest her, leaned back and closed her eyes. She calmed her beating heart and tried to block everything out, and not think about how this might backfire.

The crowd in the hallway was dispersing. She caught the eyes of a few different people who smiled in approval or gave her the thumbs up.

After a few minutes, her attorney approached and told her it was time to appear before the judge. She stood quietly as the attorneys went over the motions and the details with the judge. Suddenly, the judge turned to her and loudly stated, "the women's shelter is for women's counseling, not children's counseling. Do not take him back there. Bring with you a list of doctors in your HMO and I will choose one next time you appear. Do you understand?" Her blank stare at the judge seemed to serve as her answer.

No, no she did not understand at all. Counseling at the women's shelter was the only place that she felt her fear and terror were understood. The only place that seemed able to stop him from intimidating. The only place that tried to get Toby to understand her fear and his father's intimidating behavior. The first time it was not ignored or overlooked for the sake of diplomacy. The shelter counselor had touched on many issues with Toby that the other counselors did not, such as self blame, copy cat behavior and other Post Traumatic Stress issues. No, she did not understand that her son would have to wait until next month or longer to get help with his despondency and violence. She did not understand that he could only receive help from the next court appointed counselor until her X sabotaged it with threats, and did so without consequence. The shelter would see him tomorrow. She did not understand that the school was pleading with her to get him help and the court was tying her hands. Well, neither puts her X husband into the equation. Funny how they all seem to ignore the obvious. Was she invisible, or was it the reality of domestic violence that they could not see? She was sure that as she stood there, looking defiantly into the eyes of that judge, millions of people across the country were watching the OJ Simpson murder trial on TV. It ran in the background of her marital nightmare like a sound track. No, like an undermusic. Herbie Hanckock's Headhunter gone south. Surreal and incomprehensible and always there.

She left the courthouse without uttering another word to anyone.

I am in a house of mirrors, running. Frightened and
running. In each real and distorted image is my body
running - and my husband's face laughing. Laughing at
my flight. No, not laughing, crying. No, he is not crying.
My images in the mirrors are crying. His face expresses
no emotion after the laughter stops. No emotion, not
one. Not in one image. Not one. Not any. And I
crumble into blindness.

Counseling's end

She settled into the rocking chair in the counselor's office.
The counselor had asked to talk to Mary first, before
including the children. She had never done that before.
That, coupled with the look on the counselor's face made
Mary uneasy. She chose the rocker this time because it
meant comfort, action, movement, or at least an illusion
of all those.

Before she was seated the counselor began. "I wanted
you to know that your ex-husband was here this morning
causing quite a commotion."

"What did he want," she whispered. Her mind reeled
with a wind that blew through it with hurricane strength.
All of the pain and terror during the past five years of
counseling came rushing back to her in that storm,
throwing her down farther than she had ever been.

Noticing the change in Mary, the counselor tried to make
light of the situation, "Just to cause trouble."

Silence. Apparently, she was expected to say something.
For the life of her, she could not muster a reaction
beyond pain and horror. The counselor continued to
study her in silence.

Finally, "what trouble can he cause?" She knew
something was coming. A freight train through a dense
fog at record speed.

"Well, I don't know. He was threatening to sue us
because he says that he never agreed to allow his children
to receive counseling. I know, there is a court order. I

have it right here. I am just telling you what he said, or rather, yelled at us. He demanded to see my records. He said it was his legal right and that he would get a court order if he had to."

There it was. Train and screaming whistle both hit her, deafened her, flattened her. He was going to prevent his children from getting help. It would sure make it easier for him to manipulate them then, turn them against her. She wondered if he would ever stop trying to take the children away. She felt as if she were slipping away, loosing any fight she had left in her. She slumped down in the rocker and put her head in her hand.

"After I filed for divorce, he took everything he heard me say in marital counseling and used it against me. He took the counselors words and twisted them to fit his verbal assault. He used my family history against me in his psychological assault. When I finally accepted the fact that the marital counseling was going nowhere, I started calling the Women's Shelter hot line. I didn't know what else to do. They told me that they do not recommend marital counseling with abusive men because that this is exactly what they do. Take what they know and use it as weapons. And I thought 'why didn't the marital counselors tell me that? I just spent three years giving this guy's stockpile of ammunition.' I vowed then never to go back into counseling with him. Now it looks like he doesn't even need to be in the counseling sessions. He can get all the ammunition he wants by bullying you out of it."

Her eyes rose to meet the counselor's with this last sentence. There was silence for a moment. She could see the counselor measuring her words with great care.

For a moment, Mary's attention moved to the cliché picture on the wall behind the counselor: a mountain, a sea, a woman in white on a cliff, wind blowing her dress and scarf, white caps on the waves. She got lost in the image, lost in herself.

"I don't think that we are obligated to show him our records. But I will be honest, this has never happened to me before. My supervisor has asked me to stop treating your family until our attorneys can look at this. Trust me, I will try to have an answer for you as soon as possible. I don't know what else I can say."

She knew that she was pale. She felt pale. She felt as white as the dress being blown by the wind, as white as the tips of the waves rushing to shore. As she rose, she could not feel her body. She put all of her energy into not passing out. She did not even have it in her to cry. She was beyond tears. She had left her tears in the waves.

She knew then that she would not be back. He would prevent it, somehow. And the courts would do nothing but tell her to choose a different counselor. Someone once told her that the definition of insanity was doing the same thing over and over but expecting different results. The counseling had become the insanity.

Townhome haven

Throwing a pillow in front of the fireplace, she laid her
tired body down in front of the fire. Her friend Jim had
delivered a stack of firewood earlier today. Her firewood
angel, who worked for a tree company, told her that he
would watch the stack as he drove by and bring more
when the supply dwindled. What a blessing! She did
miss the lake and regretted having to move away from it,
but the fireplace made up for it. Fire brought her
comfort as much as water did. They meant home, joy,
and peace to her for as long as she could remember.

This town home was hers, and no one could take it away.
An oasis of peace in the middle of the chaos of her life.
She hoped to create a comfortable, peaceful home for her
children where they could celebrate life and solve life's
problems together. If she had to turn off the phone
occasionally to stop her ex-husbands constant phone
calls, that is what she would do. If she had to install a
security system tied into the police department to insure
their safety, that is what she would do. For this moment,
in front of her fire, she felt secure and sure that she
would be able to provide a wonderful home for her
children during their teenage years.

The middle school that Toby attends is one block north.
The high school that C. Jay attends is one block south.
Directly across from the townhouse was the township
park, providing basketball courts, football fields, tennis
courts, ice skating, sledding, a skate boarding area, a small
fishing pond, a small wooded area with trails and a teen
drop in center. She chose this town home because it was
the perfect location for her children. But to her, it felt like
the shelter in the woods, where she could build her fire
and welcome visitors that knew where to find her. It was
a long, hard road getting here. Breaking away from a
destructive marriage and establishing her own home, her

independence. For this moment, she felt that no one could take it away.

Inside the house she had decorated in greens, blues and silvers. The living room had a vaulted ceiling and the second floor study at the top of the stairs overlooked it. She put a lot of work into decorating on her budget. The furniture was close out priced, but very comfortable and there to be used more than admired. The effect was visually pleasing and peaceful. A place to be and become. She found a dining set at a great price that matched her mother's hutch exactly. Red maple was hard to match. She and the children ate meals at the table, with linens and a candle centerpiece. Tradition and family discussion was becoming important again.

She closed her eyes and enjoyed the silence and the warmth. The children would be home from their father's soon. She would invite them to the fireside to talk about their day. She hoped it would be the beginning of many fireside chats.

Opening her eyes, she studied the picture above the fireplace. Her framed print of Georgia O'Keefe's Black Cross New Mexico looked very different in the firelight. She marveled at the fact that it looked like a different picture entirely.

A loud knock on the door shocked her from her reverie. Her body flinched and jumped a few inches from the ground in the scare. Walking to the door she could see her X looking in the window next to it. Oh God, why couldn't he just drop the children off and leave? Her stomach turned as she wondered how she was going to stop him from throwing fits on her doorstep. Should she open the door? He looked angry and disturbed. She was not ready for a confrontation tonight.

Looking over at her reflection in the hallway mirror, she took a deep breath to steady herself. "Just walk outside, tell the children to get out of the truck and come in the house. Listen until he becomes confrontational. You do not have to fight with him. This is your house. OK, ready?" Her reflection did not look sure.

As she was holding the door open for the children to get into the house, she tried to understand what he was yelling about. She could not find an issue through the "your problem is," "this is what you always do," and "you will hear about this in court." Once the children were in the house and keeping her hand on the doorknob, she turned to him. She did not recognize him as the man she married. His face was bloated from booze and distorted from anger. What hair hadn't dropped out was graying quickly. He was dirty and unkempt. His breath was sour. She could not make sense of what he was trying to say.

"What is the issue here? What is the problem?"

"You are the problem, you - - -,"

"Did something happen tonight? Are the children all right?"

"It's not the children. You're the problem, you fucking bitch," he screamed as he moved toward her.

With that, she turned the doorknob to leave. He grabbed her shoulder and pushed her away from the door. Fear seized her as she wobbled on the step. Every violent terror came rushing back and flew through her heart one after another. Her heart beat wildly and her head whirled.

The door sprung open and C. Jay yelled, "Dad, what are you doing?" As her ex stepped back C. Jay grabbed, pulled her into the house and shut the door. She quickly locked all the locks and set the alarm.

Before she could say anything, both boys ran upstairs to their own rooms and closed their doors. So much for a fireside scene. She laid back down if front of the fire and did everything she could to slow her heart rate. How do you fight tears and slow your heart beat at the same time? You don't. The tears came and flowed for a good long time. When she was finally exhausted from crying, her heart rate had slowed and the fire had died. She wiped her tears, blew her nose, and went to bed.

Coming and going

"Dad is going to pick me up tomorrow morning at 7:30."
He looked at her directly and she could see him search
her face. It wasn't a poker face she was sure. She
struggled to formulate a calm, rational response.

"Come over here and sit down C. Jay. I need to explain
something to you." The movement cut the tension and
gave her time to think.

She arranged the pillows in the corner of the couch so
that she could lean back and rest her head while she
spoke. This was all so tiring and seemed as if it would
never end.

"Last summer, the rule was that your father was not
allowed to come here except to pick you up at the times
spelled out in our parenting agreement."

"Oh God, here we go." Hearing the frustration in her
son's voice, she proceeded with caution.

"Honey, my goal is not to make things harder on you.
My goal is to maintain as much peace as possible. I know
you don't see the harm in him coming over whenever you
want him to. Lately, he is picking you up just at the times
I leave for work and come home from work. Have you
noticed that?"

C. Jay looked down at his hands. She could tell he was
putting it together.

"You are absolutely right. There should not be a problem coming and going as you please this summer. All I ask is that your father is not here between seven and eight in the morning, and between five and six at night. That way I can leave for work and come home without worrying whether or not he is in the driveway waiting to cause a scene. My goal is no more fighting. Let's try to make that everyone's goal."

"OK mom." She could see that his hands were shaking.

"Look Cj. This is not your problem. It is nothing you are doing wrong and nothing you are responsible for. I stopped going to the door, and had the alarm system put in so that you boys have to close the door to stop the alarm. Your dad knew he could not start a fight on my doorstep anymore by forcing the door to stay open and yelling. If he did, the alarm would go off and the police would be called."

He sat back with a sigh and whispered, "I know."

"Now I think he is arranging to be here at those times to bully me or start something. I need your help with this. Just don't tell him to be here at those times. Let him come and get you or drop you off when I am not around."

She let the silence between them allow the tension to settle before she went on.

"To tell you the truth, there have been lots of times when I am leaving or coming home that I see your dad in his truck sitting on the road out there. This is a violent act, designed to intimidate me and make me feel unsafe. But I am locked in my car. I don't even look his way and it

187

doesn't bother me because I know I am safe. I don't unlock the car until the garage door has closed behind me. I don't let that bother me because it is his problem, not mine. He can't hurt me like that. Too bad he wastes his time like that."

"But now he is putting you in the middle by asking you to give him permission to be in the driveway and out of his car when I come and go. This increases the chances of a fight here. I need you to help me keep my distance from him."

This time the silence went undisturbed, until C. Jay rose with a heavy sigh and stood up. Mary too stood up to and fell into his arms for a daily hug. This one was long and strong and comforting.

"I understand Mom. Don't worry."

With that, he went up to his room and closed the door. Mary turned and went into the kitchen to prepare dinner, hoping that he did understand. Her heart broke for him.

"Donna, hold on, I'm getting a call waiting signal. The kids are here so I didn't answer at first. But this person keeps calling so I keep getting the signal. It might be a family emergency. Hold on," said Mary somewhat alarmed.

"OK," replied Donna in a uncertain tone.

"Hello," Mary said after clicking over.

"Put C. Jay on the phone." It was her X.

"Bob, I am on the other line. I will have C. Jay call you when I have finished.. Please stop calling repeatedly so that I can finish this call. I am making child care arrangements for Toby."

"I don't give a damn what you are doing. Put C. Jay on the phone right now."

"I will have him call you as soon as the phone is available." With that, Mary clicked back over to Donna.

"That was Bob, demanding to speak to the children. It is what he does whether they are eating or sleeping or in the bathroom. I told him I would have C. Jay call him when I was finished, but we might be interrupted again. If I have to ask you to repeat yourself, it is because of that call waiting signal cutting out your voice. Oh, there it is. Let's try to finish this conversation around it."

"Honestly Mayr, how do you stand it. Why can't he wait until you have finished your call. I expect better manners from my children for pity's sake!"

"Well," Mary said with a chuckle, "Bob lost his manners a long time ago, along with his morals, ethics and any integrity he had. He just is not rational. After the kids and I moved into the apartment, I had to buy phones that had a switch for the ringer so that we did not have to hear it when he called repeatedly. I tried to get the attorneys to address the subject, but it doesn't seem to be something they are concerned with. I have had the police talk to him The last one told me that they could arrest him if it happened again. Can you hear me, because I keep getting that signal?"

"Your voice keeps going in and out. I am filling in the blanks. It isn't too difficult when the story is Bob. Old story."

"Donna, I can hardly hear what you are saying. He must be calling over and over so that we keep getting that signal. Hold on and let me try to get him to stop."

"Good luck with that!"

Mary clicked over to the call waiting line. "Bob, please stop calling back so that I can finish my phone call. It is late, and I need to make these arrangements."

"You fucking bitch. Let me talk to C. Jay right now," he screamed. She could see his face in her mind, inches from her own like it had been so many times. Screaming at her. Puffed and full of rage, intimidating her.

Mary clicked over to Donna. She was now terrified and trembling.

"Mayr, are you there? What's going on?"

Mary had hesitated a moment to try to gather her wits. Fear was a button Bob knew just how to push. The tone in his voice, the aggression, the relentless intrusion into her privacy and safety sent her right into that spiral of terror that Mary could not seem to reason away.

"Oh my god, Mary. Is that him calling again? Do you want me to send Jim over there? Are you going to be OK? What is his problem this time?"

"I don't know. I can't get past the swearing and the rage. He wants to speak to the children RIGHT NOW and he won't quit."

"Didn't your children just come home from his house?"

"Yes they did."

"Well what could he have to say now that couldn't wait ten minutes. He is unbelievable."

"I don't know if he is drunk or crazy or both tonight. Let me go talk to the boys and I will call you back."

"OK. Don't forget to call. I am so upset now."

"I won't. I will call you on my cell so we can't be interrupted." As soon as Mary hung up the phone it started to ring. Instead of answering it, she went downstairs to talk to the boys.

"Your dad is calling over and over. Did you have an argument with him? Why is he upset?"

The boys were watching television. C. Jay looked up at her. "I don't know why he is upset!"

"Well, are one of you going to answer?" Neither boy moved toward the phone.

Mary waited several more phone rings and then said, "If you are not going to answer, I am going to turn off the phone." Again, neither boy moved.

Mary went into the garage to get away from the noise and called Donna back on her cell phone. After arranging drop off and pick up times for Toby while she was at work tomorrow, Mary opened the door to the garage and went back into the house. The phone was still ringing.

"OK. Now you are scaring me. What is going on here? Please talk to me."

Toby got up from his chair and said, "I'm going to bed."

Mary looked at C. Jay and said, "How about you. Can you tell me why your father keeps calling over and over? Or why he was yelling at me on the phone to put you on it?"

C. Jay looked up in exasperation. "I don't know," he cried. With that, he too ran upstairs to his room.

Mary thought to herself that she had two choices. She could pick up the phone and have her X swear and yell at her again. Or she could turn off the ringers on the phones. After turning off the ringers and the lights downstairs she walked into Toby's room.

"You OK champ?"

"Yeah," he answered from the dark. Ready for bed in record time Mary thought to herself.

"OK. If you want to talk, I will be in my room. We need to get up at 7:00 tomorrow morning to go to Donna's."

"OK mom, I love you."

Mary walked over and gave her son a warm kiss on the forehead. "I love you too baby."

After going through the same ritual in C. Jay's room, Mary returned to her own and looked at the phone. The calls were still coming in. Number eighteen, number nineteen, one after the other. When they stopped at number twenty seven, she disconnected the caller ID unit and took it downstairs.

Shivering as if she was cold, she sat in the silent darkness for a bit, trying to decide if this was one of those times to call the police. The harassment made it impossible for her to use her phone. The children could not enjoy the rest of their evening and had gone to bed depressed. Mary herself was shaking and terrified at the thought that he might come over and pound on her door like he had so many times before, screaming from the doorstop for the children to open the door.

With a heavy sign, she turned on the light and picked up her cell phone to call the police. It was going to be a long night.

Maeve's game

The hot, aluminum bleachers were beginning to stick to her sweaty legs. God, it was a hot day. The sun blared in her eyes as she sat in the stands with her friend Suzanne and tried to watch C. Jay on the football field. Players were cramping up in every play. Trainers were running water bottles onto the field for them after every play. C. Jay had not cramped yet, thank goodness.

Suddenly a face appeared inches from hers and startled her. "Hi Mary," in a high pitched, scratchy voice. She had to pull her head back to focus on the face and did not recognize it right away. It was a face that did not belong to this scene normally. A face she was probably blocking. Mary felt Suzanne move closer to her for protection.

"It's your sister!"

"Hi Maeve, I just did not expect to see you here. I had a 'what is wrong with this picture' moment."

"Bob invited us to the game since we live so close. Hot day for it though."

Maeve's face was still unbearably close and her breath was bad. She looked old and coarse, like she had smoked three packs a day for twenty years. She was probably coming off a bender. Mary looked away and saw C. Jay scrambling down the field with the ball. She stood up and yelled, "Run C. Jay run!" That backed Maeve up.

"Wow," said Maeve, somewhat put out. "Well, this is about C. Jay. That's why we're here isn't it?" Mary had her doubts about the purpose of Maeve's attendance. She had never been a football fan or particularly interested in Mary's children. Maeve was in it for Maeve, whatever it was. Mary had learned that long ago.

Since the first thing her sister did was declare the fact that she had been invited by Bob, Mary quickly surmised that Maeve's attention was to show her allegiance, and it was not to Mary. No surprise there. She never could figure out if the bond of drinking buddies was stronger than family loyalty, of if they had some financial dealings involving recreational drugs that the family was in denial about. Mary was past caring and frankly, there was really nothing she could do about their unhealthy lifestyles. The courts certainly didn't care about the effects on her children. Well, whether her sister was manipulated by her X or not, she was clearly there to stick it to Mary. This was different than the rest of her family. The rest only turned their back on the situation. Maeve was firing his guns. Well, she missed.

"So Bob tells me that C. Jay has been accepted to Harvard," Maeve shrieked. Why was she speaking so loudly? What a game this was becoming!

While she was rubbing her forehead trying to think of a courteous response, from behind her she heard "What's this, C. Jay in Harvard?"

Mary spun around and saw her friend Paul, president of the parent association for the high school. Mary chuckled, "Well, as usual, Bob's facts are askew. Harvard has been recruiting C. Jay with some other Ivy League schools. He has sent in applications but will need to get his college entrance test scores up to make the Ivy League academic index."

"Who is recruiting C. Jay?" asked Paul with a smile, shifting his glance to Maeve. Mary knew what he was really asking was "what's this?" He knew her so well. Mary shook her head with a smile to answer the implied question and continued her answer with a list of schools. With pride, Mary told the group that C. Jay was one of nine students in the state being recruited by Yale to play football.

Paul's friend Greg yelled "Go C. Jay go!" and they all looked down on the field to see number 39 fly over the goal line with the ball.

After the cheering was over, Mary turned to her estranged sister and said, "OK, you will have to check in with me after the game for any more chit chat. I will be grilled afterward so I can't miss any action." Suzanne giggled.

"Well fine," Maeve said, obviously upset. Mary did not care, how sad. It was always all about Maeve wasn't it? Well, not on Mary's time. Maeve would have to gloat somewhere else.

After her sister left, Paul leaned down and put his head on her shoulder. She reached up and patted his head without turning around.

"Long story, bottle of wine needed." He chuckled and sat back. Judy his wife breezed up and sat next to Mary.

"Why are you in the hot bleachers? You two should be underneath in the shade with us. Who WAS THAT?"

"Let's go, talk down in the shade," Suzanne pleaded.

After hearing the story, Judy proclaimed, "Well, she is just an idiot, that's all there is to it. She'd have to be an idiot to be his friend. Don't even worry about that."

"That's right," said Suzanne, giving Mary a little hug.

Paul and Judy and been two good friends that stuck by her during some terrible times. Mary met them when C. Jay was in kindergarten with their son, and the children's school activities often brought them together. Bob's contemptuous staring always bothered them at the games. They had sometimes been part of the wonderful group that surrounded Mary for protection. It turned Mary's stomach with shame to know that the community saw Bob as a town drunk, and felt the need to protect her like this. But she knew that these moments of relief from the pressure of violence that her friends provided were keeping her sane.

"Get that boy some water," Mary yelled, responding more to her own thirst than to the action on the field. She turned her face into a brief gust of wind to feel relief from the heat.

I have to tell you about the most amazing, exciting experience. C. Jay's first football conference playoff game this year was WAY downstate about six hours. I spent those six hours on the way to the game thinking about the novel I am writing and jotting notes while I drove(yes, I finally began work on that novel we talked about!) A nice break from reality. The car was a small oasis. No one could interrupt me. My world became my own for six short hours.

Needless to say I reserved a room in a local motel down there. I was delighted to find several friends had checked into the same motel. So much for any more work on the book.

Anyway, the size of crowd that traveled that distance for these kids was amazing. Our side of the stands was packed. And so was that motel, with hometown residents.

Now for the amazing part. The game was very close. In the last two minutes of the forth quarter, the other team was ahead by one point. C. Jay, our all time hero, was given the ball five times in a row to run it as far as he could, dragging many opposing players with him on each play. You could see that on each play, he ran the ball harder and went a little farther to put the ball into position for a field goal.

With each play, the crowd roared louder and the stands shook more. Everyone was on their feet, stomping and screaming. I thought the stands were going to collapse. Tears come to my eyes even now, knowing that the super human effort of my own son brought that mighty reaction from the home town fans.

Before the field goal attempt, I wisely decided to get out of the stands for my own safety. The field goal was good and Warren won the game. The bleachers did not collapse, but the crowd moved so quickly out on to the field, I was glad to be ahead of it. I was one of the first to jump the fence and run toward the team. The coach had them huddled near the goal post. By the time the huddle broke up, the crowd had pushed me very close to the players. I had a horrifying moment when the players turned and came toward me. These boy/men were immense in their football gear. And they were moving fast to find their families. I had to wonder if this is what it was like to play. I felt very small and vulnerable.

Luckily, C. Jay found me before I was crushed. He swept me up in his arms and held me until the crowd thinned out. I cannot even describe the emotions spinning around in me. Joy, mostly joy was among them. I tried to whisper to C. Jay that I loved him, but ended up having to scream it. This did not fluster him a bit. He just broke out it a great big grin and yelled his love back. Then the players, coaches and press snatched him away and he had his moment of glory. One of many in his short life.

Afterward, I found his English teacher, my friend Debra, again. I spent the game sitting/standing/screaming next to her. Her husband is one of the coaches. C. Jay has been working diligently with her at lunch time to bring up his college entrance test scores. (Remember ours?)

Anyway, I gave her a gift before leaving. Just one of those little somethings you buy for the world's greatest teacher (you probably get a lot of those.) I did not know how to thank her for everything she had done. Not only did she sit next to me while I behaved like a complete maniac during many of the games, but she spent a good part of the school year helping C. Jay with his tests and college applications. She went well beyond the call of duty. And her dedication and caring made a huge difference for my son. How do you thank someone who has given so much without thought of getting in return? Please answer me that!

Well, that is my most amazing experience. I miss you, and wish you were here to share. But thank you for staying in my life, no matter where you are.

Much love,

mmb

Get some distance

She sat on the hard, cold bench outside the courtroom. Tears were streaming down her face but miraculously, her breathing was normal and her nose was not running! It was as if somewhere a faucet had turned on by itself. She could not speak.

The State's Attorney took her hand and squeezed it. She said, "I want you to know that this verdict does not mean he is not guilty." Where had she heard that before? She lost count of how many times had heard that phrase after a courtroom hearing.

"This does not mean that his repeated phone calls were not harassment, nor does it mean that he has the right to do this. It just means that the judge did not understand completely." She thought to herself that she had rarely gone before a judge that understood.

"Why can you see what kind of man he is, and what he is doing to me and the children, but the judges can't?"

"I guess because I go against guys like this every day. But his attorneys have a pattern of getting a change of venue to a courtroom where the judge does not hear many domestic violence cases. This judge just does not have the experience to see the warning signs. And we cannot bring prior offences up in the trial."

Closing her eyes, she said "I wonder how his attorney can look himself in the mirror. Any one of the seven he has had so far!"

The State's Attorney paused and took her hand again. She opened her eyes and made eye contact. "Look, the most important thing is to keep yourself safe. Is there any possibility that you can move? The only thing that will stop this guy is distance between you. Believe me, I have seen it before."

Boom. Time stopped. Dead end. The original, really good, highly paid attorney had secured him that iron clad parenting agreement. She remembered vividly his face as he told her, "Listen, you can always go back into the court and get the agreement changed if it doesn't work out. The court will always do what is best for the children." It seemed to her that what was best for the children would be to stop their father from refusing to contribute to the medical and educational costs, from calling over and over, from pounding on the door, from screaming on the doorstep, from methodically trying to turn the children against her, from pushing her, from hitting her, from blocking her way into a room or even her own house, from belittling her in public to the shame of her children, from contemptuous staring in public, from driving around her house all the time when he knew she was leaving or coming home, or sitting in his truck across the street watching her house. But she knew now that there was nothing to stop him.

"Why do you think the judges and attorney's would think that Joint Legal Custody would work with a guy like this. I mean, he had a long history of stuff like this before the divorce hearing."

"This county gives Joint Legal Parenting as a rule if the father requests it. Unless he is found to be abusive to the children, Joint Legal Parenting is always given. The courts in this county think that it will keep the fathers in the children's lives, and that is more important than any hardship on the spouse."

"Well, my children now both suffer from post traumatic stress and depression. Doesn't that matter to the courts?"

"I know, this is the toughest appellate district in the state on this issue. It is really the worst place for a woman to get a divorce."

"Bad luck for us. How do we live through it? I can't afford to keep coming back here to keep him away from me."

"I know, all I can say is, when you think you just can't take it anymore, call the police. The State's Attorney will just keep charging him. At least it keeps him quiet for awhile. We understand what he is up to."

She felt the impact of those words tear her in two. One person stood and said, "Thank you, you have been wonderful," as she wiped away the tears. The other person closed her eyes and slipped away into darkness.

I am with my family at my moms company picnic. My mom introduces me to a coworker who is very attractive. His blue eyes look familiar, but I can't place who he reminds me of. We walk over to the tent that has the food and he makes himself a plate. I am not hungry, but we talk while he gets his food.

When I return to my family's table they have all left. I am shocked that they would leave so suddenly without telling me and feel abandon. I grab my purse and run into the woods until I can't run anymore.

A rat walks by on two feet and asks how I am feeling. When I tell him he says "What did you expect?"

This upsets me so I return to the picnic to get my car. My mom's friend stops me and insists that I eat before I go. This time while we are talking, his blue eyes are disturbing me. They look like my X's eyes.

I go to the food tent and get a plate of food to get away from him. A small woman runs up and slaps the plate from my hand. "It's poison," she screams.

I run to my car and lock myself in.

Dear Vivi,

It has certainly been a year of tremendous change for the boys and I. Through it all, we have managed to keep up and grow. We have all learned much. I hope this Christmas finds you as happy. This is the first year in several I have heard Toby say "this is going to be a good Christmas because..." We have finally come home.

It seems like I spent the entire last year consumed my job and creating our home. Much to do to make that happen and get settled. I think much of the boys new found happiness comes from having a comfortable, peaceful home once more. It has been a long journey home. We have many fireside gatherings, watching ball games or just chatting by the fire while the puppy crawls all over us. It's small but very comfortable. Home. Occasionally, while the boys are away, I have a girl's night out at my place. It would be wonderful to have you in town for one. Plenty of beds, much to catch up on.

Your letters tell me that you have had your share of change. I hope that it has served you well. And I hope that your family is all doing fine. I think of you often.

C. Jay is now driving my car more than I anticipated. So I traded in my Saturn for a full sized Chevy to fit him...6'5" with very long legs. A very big guy. Strong silent type. Great sense of humor. I'm sure you two will appreciate each other. Now that we are settled, this year has been spent finding a school for him to play football (his dream.) Possibly our alma mater, Ripon!

Toby is bright and creative. Also a terrific sense of humor. He belongs in a think tank, a real grasp of abstract concepts and psychological change. He's a great people person with much empathy.

Both boys always do their best and have terrific spirit. It's hard to believe their time with me is beginning to end. They taught me a great deal.

Oh Vivi, Merry Christmas. I love you and always will, I know it.

Please give my love to your family.

Yours always,

mmb

She looked at her mother

She looked at her mother laying on the gurney. She looked small, old and fragile. The smell of the hospital hallway turned Mary's stomach and she shifted weight from foot to foot as she took her mother's hand.

Her mother opened her eyes and smiled. "Mary Margaret, thank you for staying with me." There was a light in the smile of her eyes that reached out to Mary.

"Oh mom, it's the least I could do after all of those nights you came running to my rescue when I was having an asthma attack."

Her mother sighed, "I never knew what to do, I don't think I really helped much!"

"Mom, you did just the right things. You held me, rubbed my back, calmed me down, gave me someone to hang on to."

"Just like you are doing for me now." A stream of sweat fell down Mary's temple.

"That's right mom, just like this. I'm here because I want you to know that I love you. And I thank you for all the times that you were there for me when I really needed you. When C. Jay was born - I truly needed you then. And I thank God that I can be with you now."

"Yes, I have been thanking God too. You know, after you children were older, I was not very patient with religion. When a priest came into my room to pray, I would tell him to leave. But this time, I told the pastor that it would be all right if she said a prayer. And I was glad for that prayer. I feel very close to God now."

"Mom, you may not have been religious, but you have always taught us great lessons in faith. Honesty, integrity, work ethic, family, doing your best every minute of your life, these are the ways that you have lived your faith. And by living it, passed it along to all of your children. Thank you so much for teaching me all of these important things. They have shaped my life and my children's lives. You can be proud of my children because they also live these values that you have passed down to us."

"I am proud of your children Mary Margaret. And I am proud of you. You are such a good mother." These last words were almost a whisper. Yet they validated Mary so completely.

With that, her mother drifted off again. Mary looked over at the mirror in the waiting room and could see the strain and fatigue in her face.

As Mary waited with her mother for the medical tests, she understood the importance of this conversation. She paused a moment to enjoy the experience of her heightened senses. She closed her eyes and her mind filled with the light of her mother's love. All of her was in this moment completely. She felt every bit of the past, present and future. Colors, sounds, smells, everything was peaked. A defining moment. It was up to her to put the pain far behind. She gathered all of her strength to shut the pain out. These next hours or days with her mother would have room only for resolution, forgiveness and closure. Matters of the spirit and soul would be shared on every level. The rest was not important.

He will not be welcome

"Will Bob be attending the memorial Mary?" asked Bill,
breaking the silence filled only with her mother's labored
breathing. The breathing had become different. Each
breath took great effort, sounded loud and hard. Each
pause between breaths lasted longer and longer. Mary
knew her mother would not be drifting back from
unconsciousness again. She wondered if she was
somewhere listening to her children. Somewhere bathed
in light and peace, still courageously trying to help them
with her ending.

"No, Bob will not be attending the Memorial. It is a very
difficult situation. He was arrested last week for
disorderly conduct on my doorstep. No, he will not be
welcome." Bill gave her a blank stare. Maeve jumped up
and said, "Bill, let's go have a cigarette." They both left
the room quickly. Mary stood up slowly and asked her
brother Ken and his wife if they would be OK by
themselves for a short time. "I just need a moment to
gather myself, I won't be long" and she left the room.

As she reached down for the coke in the vending
machine she again mustered all of her strength to put the
pain and conflict behind her. The silence around her
mirrored the emptiness in her heart. She told herself that
this wasn't about her. This was her mother's end. And
she had to participate and be strong. It was important to
both of them. Her family's betrayal must not become a
part of this if she wanted resolution with her mother.
And that is what she wanted most of all.

When she returned to the room, Bill and Maeve were still
gone. Ken asked about the arrest. It felt good, the care
and concern. Interesting that the indifference comes
from the brothers and sisters who live near, who are most
able to give support but choose instead to maintain a safe

distance. As she explained the circumstances, she knew in her heart that asking for an accounting is a far reach from providing support and care. Well, someone caring enough to ask was something she wasn't used to!

As she concluded her story, and Ken and his wife voiced their concern, the room fell into silence once again. She shifted her gaze out the window at the tree outside the hospital, small and bare and frail. She wondered if it would survive the winter. Closing her eyes, she focused again on her mother's breathing. She struggled to gain a perspective needed for strength and peace. She struggled to quiet the silent scream that echoed through her mind. Her brothers and sisters were all products of the same family that led her to her own choices. She could not blame them. She needed to forgive them. And this was a time of forgiveness. She felt the calm spread over her with the sound of her mother's breathing.

Mom's last breath

When Bill came back into the hospital room after having a cigarette with Maeve, he brought his wife and children. The children sat quietly for a while, clearly uncomfortable about being apart of their grandmother's death. Mary began to try to include them in the conversation. She asked about school and athletics. The discussion came around to   C. Jay and Toby and football. "Have I told you my story about the Chicago Bears Mini Camp?" The children in unison said, "no."

"Well, I will have to wake up a little to tell this one," said Mary as she sat up from her laying position in the recliner. She could see her own tired face in the mirror across the room. The two hours sleep she managed the night before in the most uncomfortable chair at her mother's side were wearing on her. The light in the room was changing with the dusk and helping the weariness along.

Mary spun the yarn about her family adventure at the Chicago Bear's mini-camp last season. About the tour through the new Bear's facility, the catered luncheon, which players the children met and how excited they were. She told about how C. Jay inconspicuously took a football from a bag on the sidelines after the team had finished practice and begun throwing it to Toby, running all over the field. She told about how afterward, as they went back to the tent so the boys could get dessert, a very nice gentleman from the Bears approached her, and started a conversation. When she brought him over to introduce him to the boys, she could only mention their names because he never told her his name. After showing genuine interest in the boy's football careers, he was whisked away by a co-worker. She told the family that the boys made fun of her when she said, "Well he was a nice guy wasn't he?" and they realized she did not know that he was the new head coach.

As her story ended, she heard Ken, who was at her mother's bedside, let out a heavy sigh. She looked at her mother and realized that she had stopped breathing. This was the end. The end of a long journey. She had been completely immersed in this process for days. The last 36 hours, she rarely left her mother's side. Every part of her screamed with the fatigue and the beauty of a peaceful ending.

Now it was over. All of her mother's children had been with her at the end. She had taken great pains to make sure that everyone was at peace with her passing. Ken, the oldest, who had not arrived to see his mother conscious, had been holding her hand and stroking her forehead at her last breath. She held on until he arrived and gave him the final connection.

She looked around the room and noticed that people had begun to cry and hug. It seemed as if they were all moving in slow motion. She went to get the nurse to give her the news. Then she walked down the hall to catch her breath and compose herself.

Afterward, when everyone else had gone, she and Maeve stayed to pack their mother's things and make the final arrangements with the hospital. "What will happen to her now? Should I stay until they come to take her from the hospital?" Mary asked the nurse. She could still hear her mother's breathing in her ears. It only stopped when she looked at her mom and saw that she was not taking a breath. The breathing echoed in her ears like a primal scream.

When should she leave her mother? Mary was not prepared for this moment. She did not know what she believed about life directly after death. Was her mother still near? Did she need her to stay and pray? Did she need her to let go so she could move on? In all of the intensity of the past few days, all of the decisions of spirit that allowed her to share her mother's death, she had not anticipated this moment and was not prepared for it.

"I can't stay," cried Maeve as she burst into tears. Mary knew then that her mother would want her to take care of her sister.

She kissed her mother's cheek and rubbed her hand for the last time. With tears streaming down her face, she left the hospital room whispering, "Bye mommy."

Leaving the memorial with Donna

Laughing with the children felt good. She felt the fear and anger of the past hour subside as she looked into the faces of the youngest generation of her family, so beautiful, reaching out to her. It was like looking at her own reflection. She sadly wondered in what manner, the family legacy of alcoholism and violence would be passed on to them. She was sure it would be.

Behind her, a familiar voice, "There you are!" She turned around to see her friend Donna's daughter Amanda, peaking through the crowd at her. Mary's smile eased the tension in Amanda's face as she ran up and hugged her. Donna was not far behind and reached also to give her a warm, generous hug. "I can't believe he is here," Donna said as Mary pulled back to look at Donna's face. Her quiet voice screamed compassion and instantly reconnected Mary.

"It happened just as you predicted. Mauve gave Bob all the information and here he is, in spite of what I told my family in the hospital."

"I can't believe your family. What did you do?"

"Well, first I asked Mauve if she had invited him. She told me that he called her for the address and she gave it to him. When I asked her if she thought that it was her decision to make, whether Bob attend or not, she told me that she felt it was his decision to make. I asked if it occurred to her that he should have gotten the information from me, which of course, he had not done. She said no. I said well, let me tell you what happened when he walked in the door! He walked right up to me, looked me up and down a couple of times with an intense anger in his eyes, made a loud scoffing noise, and then walked by me to my children. My children were watching – and yours may have been too! Mauve jumped up and started making a scene saying 'I'm not going to get into this now!' So much for family support. C. Jay and I left to get something to eat. Toby would not leave. I think he was afraid that something might happen to his dad. Doesn't look like anyone here cares enough for that to happen."

Mary looked over at Amanda who looked frightened and unhappy.

"Let's forget about him, let me show you the pictures of my mom. We put together a great history for her send off."

As Donna's family and Mary walked to the memorial pictures, Donna tugged on Mary's arm. "Did you see the way he looked at you, God, he is still staring at you with that creepy look." Donna's husband Jim added, "When you walked by, he looked you up and down several times. If someone looked at Donna like that I'd have to take him out."

"Apparently no one else here cares about how he looks at me, except maybe my children who are traumatized. Just ignore him for now. I will be leaving shortly. Hopefully, that's how it will end."

They looked at the pictures of her mother.

"She looks so much like you."

"Thank you, she was very beautiful." Mary looked intently at the family mirror.

"God Mary, I have to leave, I can't stand the way he keeps looking at you with all of these people around. Why doesn't anyone do anything?"

"What I have learned about my family is, they just don't have a clue. Come on, I will say my good byes and leave with you." She wiped a tear from her cheek as she walked toward the door holding Donna's hand.

Walking to the car with her children she held her head high and whispered, "Bye Mommy."

I am on a long stretch of sandy beach with Meg and I have lost my purse. Once in awhile Meg will call me over thinking she has found it but it turns out to be a false hope. I am frantic to find my purse because my keys, pictures and wallet are in it.

We are on an island somewhere but I don't know why. Suddenly Meg disappears and I am alone. A feeling of dread fills me and I am convinced I will never find my purse. I return to a small cabin where I can sleep. I turn out the light in the bedroom and draw the curtains, removing light from the room.

I lay down on the bed and cry myself to sleep.

Desperately seeking Suzanne

She looked down at the card in disbelief. The envelope had been opened and taped closed again. In Suzanne's handwriting on the envelope she read, "I opened this by mistake." She sat down slowly in the nearest chair, feeling like she was just punched in the stomach, knocking the air from her.

She remembered sending this card to Suzanne after hearing that she had donated her kidney to a friend. Suzanne abruptly ended their friendship without offering a reason a several months ago. Mary would still, from time to time, send her a card. Times like Christmas, a family birthday or an illness were when she missed her friend most. They were there for each other for several years as neighbors and friends. Facing the sometimes wonderful, sometimes cruel world together. Mary never received an answer to her cards but hoped to someday. She just wanted to let Suzanne know she was there from time to time. She did not understand the personal politics behind Suzanne's need for distance. She hoped that Suzanne would change her mind after getting a card someday. Until now. Now it seemed that hope was gone.

She suddenly felt uncomfortable sitting. She felt the need for fresh air. After a long sigh, she lifted her aching body and moved up stairs. She glanced briefly in the mirror by the door and thought how strange she looked. A stranger. Unconnected.

After entering her bedroom she opened both windows as far as possible. The air was cold, but she didn't care. The cold air kept her from slipping away somehow. She took her shoebox filled with old greeting cards and sat down in the down filled chair. The chair she used to nurse her children. The chair that supported so much joy and comfort. Supported life and gave life. If only it could do that now.

She opened the cards from Suzanne one by one and read them.

Dear Mary,

I'm not sure I would have found the strength to get through the past couple of weeks without my "angel" reassuring me that mine was "a position of strength." Thank you for your love...for your reassurance...most of all, for just being you. You've given new meaning to "best friend" and I love you.

Suzanne

Dear Mary,

As this year ends and the new is upon us, I feel blessed to have a friend like you. Perhaps you are the best that happened to me this year. It was so good to talk yesterday and empty the contents of my heart to someone who would understand and accept and love. You have touched my life in a way it hasn't been touched in a long time. I had this empty space in my heart, and you and your love have filled it.

Thank you for making a difference in my life...for helping restore my faith in the power of friendship and the joy therein. Most of all, thanks for being you--a warm, wonderful, kind, sensitive, loving spirit who is willing to share that with me.

I love you,

Suzanne

Mary took a moment to remember the warm, colorful closeness she once had with Suzanne. She had not opened herself so intimately to anyone since Suzanne turned away. She didn't have a friend to hold her while she cried like Suzanne did so many times. She missed that. She would sometimes dream that someone was holding her while she cried, but it was never Suzanne in her dream. In fact, she could not remember recently dreaming about Suzanne at all. The loss was probably still too painful. C. Jay would occasionally come and hold her if she cried for a long time. She wasn't sure that was healthy. But she was grateful for it. She read on:

Dear Mary,

Sometimes having a friend like you makes all the difference. It surely does to me! Thank you for listening and for comforting when I can't seem to turn off the tears. You're the best.

I love you,

Suzanne

She and Suzanne really had held each other through divorce. Each divorcing for different reasons. Each trying desperately to help their children through the trauma. Each suffering the pain of divorce a little less because they could share with the other.

Mary,

"Friendship is the relationship we all need to help us through our other relationships..." Thanks for your friendship and love. Your presence in my life is a blessing.

I love you,
Suzanne

She remembered her shock when she discovered that Bob had taken Suzanne's cards from her dresser and copied them during the divorce. Her attorney presented the copies to her and told her Bob had claimed that she was having a lesbian affair. These cards with all of their "I love you" were to prove that. She laughed for the first time in a week, thinking about it.

Then the cards with the mixed messages, sent while Suzanne was turning away:

Dear Mary,

Yours is one of the many pieces I have dropped over the past few weeks. I haven't been here for you and I do apologize and hope that our friendship has not suffered because of my selfishness. I do love you and our relationship, and I believe you understand my actions and in your ever gracious way, have forgiven me for slighting you.

I love you,
Suzanne

Dear Mary,

On Saturday when I decided to stay home and finish the
job I had started (cleaning her bedroom), I obviously did
not intend to hurt and/or upset you. But it seems I have.
Your friendship has been something I have cherished.
You have helped me over, around and through some of
the worst times in my life. If my actions have hurt your
feelings, I apologize. I'm anxious to hear how things
went with the mediator on Saturday. I hope you'll want
to share that with me.

I love you,
Suzanne

Dear Mary,

Sometimes, I simply feel like wrapping you in a huge hug
and holding you forever. I want to always be here for
you.

I love you,
Suzanne

Dear Mary,

I just wanted to remind you that I love you. I'm sorry I
made you feel as thought something was wrong. You're a
wonderful friend.

I love you,
Suzanne

Darkness was falling and it was becoming difficult to read. Letting all of the cards fall to the floor, she nestled back into the down chair and ottoman, covering herself with the blanket. She wondered briefly about all of the mixed messages at the end of the relationship. What was their purpose? Closing her eyes, she told herself that she didn't care, it was too late to care. Where did that part of herself go that she had given to Suzanne? It had seemed so real and wonderful at the height of the friendship. Now it was probably somewhere turning into something she would not recognize, like her image at the courthouse. What happens to people who don't recognize their own spirit? It seemed as if everything she felt inside was not at all real outside. Loosing all connection, inside out. Outside in was completely unfamiliar. Lost, all lost as she slipped away into darkness and sleep.

The announcement

It was as if she was suddenly watching herself from above. She could see her own face, relaxed with a courteous smile. She heard her heart was beating furiously in her chest, but could not feel it.

Her boss watched her cautiously for a moment before he continued. "I think that this is a great opportunity for me and my family. It will shorten my retirement timeline considerably. We will move to Vegas for a few years, and can move back then after the job is over and I retire. Being away from my children and friends will be hard, but we will come back every month or so for a weekend." He paused again. She heard herself say, in an amazingly warm tone, "That's great! I'm so happy for you. What a rare opportunity!." He paused again, looking at her closely before beginning again. She quickly added with honesty "I'm sad for me, but happy for you!"

Her boss was leaving the township. His replacement was yet to be determined.

She couldn't hear the rest of what he was saying but she could see herself responding in a way that made him more comfortable. Time stopped because the future was suddenly black and terrifying. She had found the job she knew would stabilize her, even make her happy. Suddenly, it all vanished. The uncertainty was overwhelming and divided her into two people. The person she needed to be, and the person that was slipping away - evaporating like dew on a summer day with nothing to cling to but unstable, unreliable air. The air was changed with every contact it made - nothing to see or hold. That slipping away person fell into the darkness where she would wait until she remembered how to breathe.

Lost on familiar streets

As she drove along in the car, her mind was completely inside the song coming from the radio. *Can't Stay Away From You* by Gloria Estefan brought bittersweet pictures of Toby to mind. She unconsciously put her driving on automatic pilot and sang the tune of the song as she drove.

Suddenly, she realized that she did not know where she was. As she looked around, she did not recognize the streets, the buildings, not anything! Her heart began to beat furiously and she quickly turned off the radio and tried to get her bearings. Oh my God, had she taken a wrong turn? She was only going to work. She should recognize something!

As her panic grew her driving slowed. The car behind her honked. The sound startled her and increased her panic. Tears began pouring down her cheeks.

She said to herself out loud, "Breathe. Calm down. Keep driving. You will recognize something eventually. You are not that far from home!" Her voice sounded to her like a scream, but the beat of her heart drowned it out.

As she crossed over the bridge she realized where she was. About a mile from home on her usual route to work. She sat back in her seat as calm slowly rushed over her. She pulled off to the shoulder, stopped the car and closed her eyes to regain clarity.

This was not the first time she became suddenly lost on streets that she had driven for 20 years. The stress of everything was getting to her. She would need to just relax and will it all away. She briefly wondered if she should go back to counseling. But that had always turned into such a disaster. Either he found a way to interfere or acting on the advice only escalated her problems. No, she would just need to be strong and get herself through this.

She turned the radio back on to end the silence. She listened briefly to the Beatles *Carry That Weight* before turning it off again. Resolving not to tell anyone about this, she resumed her drive to work. This would be just another one of those things to tuck away and bear alone.

I need to share my wonderful, bittersweet night with you. Telling you all about it in my head just won't do this time. I had a rare and incredible mom night. One that comes along once in a lifetime.

After a grueling and very painful root canal in the morning, my mouth was throbbing by evening. I finally gave in and took a pain pill about 8:00 PM. C. Jay arrived at 8:20 PM, wanting to talk about the college decision that he needed to make by tomorrow.

By then the pain was gone so we dove right into careful decision making, looking at all the good and bad points of his top ranked colleges. We talked with a passion. When we needed a break from analyzing the decision, we talked about school, friends, morals and spirituality, possible graduate school - many huge important things.

We talked at length about the negotiation process and what it took to get these final packages. On his end, entering the Presidential Scholarship competition at the University of Chicago and putting the effort into recruitment there set the benchmark for financial aid packages. On my end, negotiating in good faith with kindness and courtesy but most of all persistence, using my leverage points and accessing others. In the end, it was all C. Jay's hard work studying and re-testing to bring those scores up. Getting up and going to those tests early Saturday morning after the late Friday night football games, being tired and sore and all beat up. I made sure that he knew it was all of his effort in testing and maintaining his grades brought him to this point, which was choosing Yale.

We talked and talked. And when he made his decision about 10:15 we talked some more and hugged a lot. At 10:40 I walked him to the door, exhausted. He had his coat and shoes on ready to go to his dad's for the night. During our last hug he added, "maybe I should stay and take a shower." As he was removing his jacket he spread his arms and said "This is the most I have ever talked in my life." That brought tears to me and more hugs as I said, "Well I'm glad it was with me."

We went upstairs, I got into bed, he danced around my room and we talked until 12:30 AM. He never did take that shower. At 12:25 he looked at the clock and said "I have to go - I have to be on time to school in the morning."

What a great night. A stand out mom night. I know that he is happy and relieved. He talked all the way out the door, my quiet C. Jay. I imagine he talked to himself all the way to his dad's.

After he left, the silence fell over me like nightfall. I realized that my son had filled my life in the past twenty years the way he filled my home with conversation tonight. With passion and excitement and wonder and love. Once gone, the darkness fell with an unexpected heaviness that squeezed all of the air from my spirit. I am so happy for him. I know he will shine. How will I live without that brilliance? It will be gone so suddenly after 20 years. Gone like the closing of the door and silent aftermath. Or is it after birth? One last push when my aching heart has already taking all the pain it can stand. I delivered it twenty years ago, but can't remember how. I remember the pain. I remember the joy of his entrance into my life. The joy of finally being able to see him and hold him and hear him. Where will the joy be this time, after this final push out into the world to complete his delivery? I cannot imagine daily life without him.

Thankfully, after this wonderful and weighty experience, sleep came to me though the silence, allowing my spirit to breathe again.

God Vivi, sometimes I'm so afraid.

mmb

He says he knocked gently

Waiting for the State's Attorney to return, she tapped her fingers on a hard cold bench in the hallway of the courthouse. This was the first time she had been removed from the courtroom for his testimony. A new twist in court room tactics. More comfort for the victim. Not.

After a long, nerve wracking wait, the two, young, State's Attorneys returned. She could tell be their faces that it had not gone well for her in there. She did not expect it would. He had again, hired the most expensive, aggressive law firm in the county. How did these guys live with themselves?

"I see it did not go well for me."

"No, he was found not guilty. We're very sorry. We know what you have been through."

The truth was, they knew of one grain, in the harvest silo that was her experience of domestic violence.

But they were young, and kind, and she was sure they had done their best against one of the counties most seasoned defenders of societal slime.

"Well, I am sure that you did your best. Thank you. So, what did he say? How did he explain himself?" After they paused and looked down, she added, "Did he say he knocked gently, and politely asked to see his son?"

They both looked up in amazement. "That is exactly how he presented it! He even demonstrated a knock!"

She began laughing and crying at the same time. They both became very uncomfortable.

"So it really doesn't matter what actually happens, as long as there is no witness to prove otherwise."

"Well, basically yes. And this kind of guy will usually make sure there are not witnesses. We could have called your children in, but I am sure you understand the problems there."

Did she ever. "Yes," her voice whispered, but wanted to scream. "Truthfully, I could not picture any other outcome."

One of the attorneys sat next to her and took her hand. "We know this is difficult for you. And we don't want you to stop calling the police when you need to. The State's Attorney's office decides whether or not to bring your case to trial. Our office knows his past. We will be there again next time to help you."

Again she laughed. "I don't mean to be rude, but are you guys trained to say that?"

They both blushed and said, "yes."

"Look, I don't mean to embarrass you. You have been very kind and done your best. Thank you both."

"Take care of yourself, Mary."

"I'll try."

Goodbye C. Jay

Standing by the door, looking out the window, she could feel her little dog moving near her ankles, trying to get a look at the truck carrying C. Jay off to school. Through the trees, she watched the truck drive off. It looked as if it were driving on the tree branches instead of the road as her tears blurred the perspective. Her whole being was locked into the physical - the soft tickle of the dog's hair on her legs, the rumble of the truck driving off, the light of the twilight sky, the smell of the sparerib dinner (his favorite) mixed with chocolate cake dessert still in the air.

She stayed frozen at the window for quite a long time after the truck was out of sight - frozen and blank.

She came to her senses as she noticed her reflection in the window, a mirror image of her blank expression. With a heavy sigh, she breezed into the living room and fell into a chair.

As she began to sort out her feelings, a series of flashback memories rushed across her mind spontaneously:

❖ C. Jay first born in the hospital, bright eyed, so strong he held his head up from the very first day

❖ Cuddling at naptime after reading Dr. Seuss

❖ dressed like the strong man on circus day in nursery school, so proud of his role

❖ swimming with Tom on beach day

❖ receiving his black belt in Tae Kwon Do

❖ playing hockey on the lake with the summertime gang during the Christmas holiday

❖ graduation from grade school

❖ hugging her in his football uniform after the best game of the season

❖ his excitement at the state final varsity basketball tournament

❖ getting ready for dances

❖ winning the All Conference and National athletic awards

❖ the National Honor Society ceremony

❖ all of his daily hugs

❖ all the times he held her when she cried

❖ the times he cared for her when she was sick, even when he was so young

❖ his bright, understanding smile

A feeling of happiness swept across her and was then gone. She was so happy for C. Jay, beginning his life again on his own terms. Living his dream of playing college football. The thought of his strength and integrity made her smile. And she hoped to come back to this very spot each time she thought of him in his absence. This was all about him, and his future. She knew that and struggled to put her own feelings aside. And when the happiness left, only the struggle remained. With C. Jay gone, and Toby staying at his father's more and more, her struggle became her loss. And she wondered if she had the strength to overcome.

I will not be back

"That's very kind of you, but I will not be back." She knew her hands were trembling. She felt as if every ounce of energy had been drained from her. She could not bring herself to look her attorney in the eye. Because she found herself wishing that her life would end.

"Look, Mary, I mean it. I am worried about you. You can't let this guy get to you like this. I know it cost you more in my fees to recover the money he owed you, but I don't know how we could have avoided that. He is the children's father, good or bad. Sure, he has been a jerk in the courthouse. But you are over reacting. I do not understand why you are so upset."

With a sigh that let out all her breath, she rose from her chair and wobbled a bit. She did not know how to respond to that. For ten years she had been doing this. Attorneys, judges, courtrooms, tears, anger, despair, all elements of this room with no exit. For two years from the time she filed for divorce she was trapped in the same house with him. No one and nothing could stop the violence. It took three years after that to settle the property and by that time, she owed everything to the attorneys. Five more years of family court and domestic violence court because of the continued abuse. It would never stop. And no one cared.

Mary was forced to find a new attorney since her original attorney retired after representing her for nine years. She was sure that he climbed a few rungs in the Karmic ladder by sticking with her. Her new attorney only knew the abbreviated history that Mary had time to give her. Her promise to collect the back child support and get a court order for her X to pay all attorney fees turned into months of court action and more debt for Mary.

"I can't stop this guy from getting to me, and apparently, neither can anyone else in this world. But we did try didn't we? Or did we? Was there something else I could have done? Just what is it I'm doing wrong? I know you don't have any answers. Neither do I."

The silence between them should have impelled her to leave. Instead, she lost herself in her attorney's eyes. She forgot where she was and what she was supposed to do next.

"What will you do?" said her attorney, not knowing what else to say.

"Do? I have been told that I have done everything I can possibly do. I guess that means there is nothing left to do. Do, what a funny word!" She realized that she was no longer making sense. She whispered goodbye and walked slowly out of the courthouse.

As she walked outside, the noise of the city screamed at her. Life screamed at her. And she could not muster a whisper to reply.

They lay head to head on a shared pillow in front of the fire light. All other lights off. No sound but the sounds of their voices as they explored their spirits. Each watching the fire, they tried their best to understand the meaning of disappointment, together.

She passed the bottle of ice water to her son. He sipped it slowly, and she could almost feel the relief of his thirst with each sip.

"I am not a hero. I lost the game for my team."

"Toby, you did not lose that game. Football requires team effort. One player cannot lose a game. Your coaches call the plays. They decided to give you the ball again and again. The officials made their calls. The other players block or not. You had nothing to do with any of that. But your effort was heroic and inspiring to everyone playing and watching. Everyone was amazed at how much effort, strength and determination you put into those last few plays. And when you wept afterward, we wept with you because we knew that you gave everything you had to win that game for your team."

"Your effort was heroic. No matter what the result, win or lose, that effort was amazing. That is why you are a hero. And not just mine, but everyone's. You can't win every game. But if you keep playing that hard and with that much heart, you will be an outstanding player."

"You are an outstanding player. And an outstanding person. You were born with a golden heart as big as Texas and you have never lost touch with it. That heart, with all of its strength and kindness and sensitivity to people is what makes you my hero. Always has and always will."

"Winning the game would have been more exciting. It would have given you glory. But your effort would have been the same. Winning would not have made you more of a hero. Because it was your effort that was heroic. Winning would have eliminated the disappointment, but it wouldn't have changed your strength of character, how you played that game with your whole heart and put everything you had into it. Win or lose, that stays the same. The fact that you are a hero."

She spoke slowly to allow the fire light to work its magic. The top of her head tingled where it was touching her son's. Tingled from the sharing and love.

As she paused, Toby let out a long heavy sigh. The crackle of the fire became the only sound.

"I love you mom."

"I love you too baby, with all my heart."

I am walking through a cemetery slowly, looking for a headstone shaped like an elephant. Many of the flowers and plants on the graves are dying. They remind me of the fact that I have cancer. I wonder if my insides look like the dying gardens.

I pass a grave that has a coffin unburied. I suddenly notice Toby standing behind this grave. I begin to walk toward him but the closer I get to him, the more he disappears. Before I can reach him he vaporizes into the evening mist.

Goodbye AJ

She stopped for a moment before entering the funeral home. She took a deep breath and closed her eyes. Her own image appeared in her mind's eye in soft focus, her image as a teenager, long hair, and no make up. As she smiled at herself she felt in her hands her parting gift. Opening her eyes, she looked down at the tiny frame around the words, "every child is a gift." Releasing the breath from her lungs, she moved herself into the building and was startled by the crowd in the lobby. She moved through the sea of unfamiliar faces to the coat rack in the rear. As she slowly removed her coat and hung it she looked at herself in the mirror on the wall. A tired, old, sad face looked back at her, certainly not the face conjured moments before. Turning, she noticed a long line of people streaming into the viewing room. Her emotions rang together like church bells and she realized that she may not be prepared for what was to follow.

Another deep breath and she ducked into the side door behind the fire fighter's Honor Guard standing there. While they lined up to march at attention and change the guard next to the small casket she slipped into one of the hundred chairs arranged in the center of the enormous viewing room. The only dry eyes in the room belonged to the firemen, who stood motionless and straight on either side of the coffin.

The crowd parted and as she peeked through it, time stopped. Silence enveloped her and a tunnel of moving color surrounded a small child's face laying motionless at the front of the room. Her heart beat filled her ears and a long, deep sigh brought the sounds of the room back to her as time resumed in slow motion. The crowd sounds blended, and she realized that the AJ she knew as active and joyful lay lifeless, uncovered. He passed away abruptly from sudden onset of juvenile diabetes. Gone in a heartbeat before she could grab one more smile.

She looked down at her gift for him. "Every child is a gift." It hung near the door of the nursery since C Jay was born. It remained when the crib was removed and the room became Toby's. It meant welcoming new life, treasuring childhood, honoring the short time a parent has with a child. Who can expect that time to be only 11 years? Who is prepared for the sudden and tragic ending? She wanted AJ to have it now. She wanted to honor the joy he brought to all who knew him. But she could not move from her chair to bestow her gift. Well, wait and watch. She decided to give herself time.

Katie and Jeff stood next to the coffin. Next to each of them were their new spouses. She had been so angry at Jeff for walking out on Kate, for having a long term affair before finally admitting that it was time for him to go, for tearing his family apart to suit his own needs. Now she saw in him only pure pain, top to toe, heart to soul. She could feel only compassion. Katie stood next to him and comforted everyone who came to her, especially the children, patting and rubbing them, letting them know that AJ had gone with God in his time, showing her amazing strength.

She watched people circling through the room, past the parents, past the coffin and the Honor Guard. She watched the tears and the pain and the grief. She had no idea how she herself would be able to make that journey, around the room, outside of time, to the core of the heart. She knew that now, her legs would not carry her. She continued to wait.

She could see Jeff and Katie looking over at her time and again. Sitting there for an hour and a half alone must have seemed odd. When her mind began to scream, she would pray and focus. When her mind began to wander, she would see AJ's laughing face, see him rolling in the grass before her as she tickled him.

She introduced herself to Katie's mother who was walking by and tried to describe her admiration of Katie's strength. It didn't help to calm her. She felt like a babbling idiot as she spoke and her legs would not lift her from her seat to shake hands. After that, she gave up trying to be social and concentrated on pulling her strength together and moving to AJ to bid farewell. Good bye to that blithe and beautiful spirit.

The queue of visitors disappeared. The evening was ending. Katie's eyes moved back to her. It was the strength in those eyes and not her own that finally lifted her from her chair. " Mary" Katie sang as she approached them. A strong but gentle embrace brought tears to her eyes. "You are my hero" she whispered in Katie's ear. She turned to Jeff who immediately put his big arms around her and began to sob. "He knows you love him," she repeated to him several times. "I don't know what to say, I'm so sorry," was all she could muster for the new spouses.

Reaching AJ's casket she felt a terrible thirst. Her throat closed as she swallowed to find her voice. The room melted to flowing color and only that small, lifeless face came into focus. "Go with God little AJ," she whispered as she put her gift beside him. A young girl that had walked up next to her took her hand and squeezed it. Life and time began to fold in on her. No sight, no sound, no breath left. She turned and walked away hoping not to fall apart. The harder she tried to hold herself together, the faster she walked. She could see nothing, hear nothing. She couldn't breath as she walked faster, moving where? Out- she did not know what was guiding her, moving faster and faster. She vaguely heard a voice "Amanda, grab her." Flying past the coat rack she grabbed her coat and the faces of concerned fire fighters came into focus. She pleaded with herself to hold it together until she was alone in her car and the silence.

As she turned to leave she felt a hand on her shoulder. "Mary," a familiar voice filled her heart and she embraced comfort while allowing herself to finally sob. Let go, let tears flow. When time again began she realized that Amanda was now also sobbing. "I'm so sorry, I didn't mean to bring anyone else into my tears. No matter how I tried, I couldn't stop them." As Amanda's face came into focus she whispered, "But I am glad it was you." Amanda smiled through her tears, "me too." More tears inside the long embrace.

I was so sorry to hear about your father's death. He was always kind to me while we were growing up. And he was so wonderful with C. Jay (and me) in the 5 years that he was our pediatrician. Always so happy to see us and show me what a great baby I had.

I will never forget the wonderful tricks that he showed me, like C. Jay's perfect balance, even before the baby could stand or sit. And his sage advise when he found out that I made baby food from organic fruit, vegetables and grains: "Mary, he is not a science project." I did love your father. I was so sad when he retired right before Toby was born. He would have loved Toby too. And been a great comfort in my zombie phase through Toby's colic.

I know what you mean about the grieving rituals and how surreal they can be. When I was in pre-divorce counseling, the counselor asked me why I did not visit my father's grave site. I honestly did not know. I had never felt the need. The counselor asked me to pay dad a visit and let me know what happens. I found dad's grave, right next to his mother who was next to his father. I did not remember them all being together. In fact, I have no memory of my father's funeral at all, which is odd. But after all, it happened over twenty years ago.

I placed a pebble on the headstone and said hello. The counselor told me that it was a Russian tradition to put pebbles on the headstones. Why not? I chose one that I had kept since college for sentimental reasons. I told myself that maybe it would help my dad feel me there.

I really did not know what I was doing there or what I was supposed to feel. I sat down, leaned up against his headstone and looked up at the clouds going by. I thought about my grandparents immigration from Ireland to Highland Park and how difficult that must have been. I wondered what it was like to grow up in Highland Park a child of immigrants. I thought about dad's military career and college days. I marveled at his strong, unwavering faith. He may have been whispering his love to me, I think I felt that. It was a beautiful warm day and as I lay in the sun's light I think I even dozed off for awhile. I'm sure I was quite a sight, not the usual graveside visitor.

I told the counselor at my next visit that I knew I should probably have been sad, but really wasn't. I told him about all of the thoughts I thought. I asked if he thought I had an issue with my father's death that I had not faced. He said no, I seemed to be doing just fine.

We all find closure and experience loss differently. I did not attend the little ceremony that Shawn hosted for my mother. The family spread mom's ashes in her rose garden at home as she requested. I felt that I had reached closure in the hospital with my mom. And my family was such a pain in the ass at the wake, no need to go there again.

I know you will find your way through this. I am here for you.

mbc

He is their father

"Hi, this is Mary. I got your letter with the motion from my X requesting residential custody of my youngest son. Does he really think that the court will do this after all the orders he has violated? Doesn't he need a foundation for this? Does he think the court will just ignore all of the counselor reports that explain his history of alienating my son from me? Those reports are right there in the permanent court record. Doesn't anyone ever read the documents in that file? Can he really just hire an expensive attorney and drag me into court whenever he wants to? Doesn't he think anyone will remember all the crap he has pulled? Doesn't any of this need to make sense to the judge? I'm a good mom. Can he take my son away? Let me know what your retainer will be and I will see what I can do. Thanks."

She hung up the phone and pulled the bed covers over her head to lose herself in darkness. The only sound was the wind rattling the windows above the bed. If only that would really make the world go away. She had given up hope of the world making sense anymore. She just wanted it to go away.

The letter from her attorney included a copy of a Petition to Change Custody filed by her ex-husband. Her first message to her attorney was simply a whisper, "How can he do this?" Her attorney had called back and replied, "He is their father." Did that justify the abuse and strain on their lives? She did not understand how the courts could continue to facilitate it.

Suddenly she remembered Toby's counselor predicting that her X would increase his effort to alienate Toby from her once C. Jay left for college. At the time she thought that she could handle it. She did not think that it would take the form of another court battle. Would the financial drain bankrupt her? She knew she was not physically strong enough to work more. Getting a second job was out of the question. Her health was bad enough right now with all the stress. God, how could the court system possibly allow this? The system seemed to support this abuse.

She knew she could not defend herself without losing in court. His attorney was the most aggressive and expensive in the county. To give up custody would be just like abandoning her son.

Would he ever graduate high school living with dad? At dad's, he was never expected to do homework and it didn't matter whether he went to school or not. He had missed 10-15 days of school each year during his dad's residential time since grade school, putting him at a very high risk to drop out of school. He was tardy 57 days in 8th grade, a school record, Toby would proudly boast. The court refused to look at all of that.

There was no way she could afford to keep her home, help pay for college, and pay for a court battle.

If she gave up, and let Toby go, would he ever forgive her? Could she ever forgive herself? Would it cause a rift between the boys? If Toby didn't graduate high school or drank his way through life like his father, what would become of him? Would not going to court mean a future of darkness for her son? Giving up would be the easy thing. Would it be the right thing?

Toby's dad became the extreme Disney Land Dad during the teenage years. First there was the classic, expensive car built for the drag strip (birthday present on his 15th birthday, before he had a drivers permit). Then the $5,000 a year in pocket money (a fact her X proudly presented the last go round in court.) What 15 year old boy wouldn't choose having all that and doing just what he pleased with it? Mary did not enter into a competition of affection. But her son took the bait and now refused to come home, saying only that he could "do what he wanted at Dad's."

The fact that the courts would support the alienation and lifestyle and allow her son to choose tore her in two. One part grieved for her youngest son. The other raged against herself for ever thinking that love and truth could keep him close.

The state's attorney had said that only distance between them would stop her X's abuse. If she sold her home and moved away without Toby she may find peace in her life. Could she forgive herself for leaving him? Did he understand what he was doing, or was his father's domination now part of who he was to become? Could she change anything? Did she have the energy to try? Or would the stress of trying kill her?

Would she have to choose between her health and home, and her son? The thought made her blood run cold. What kind of person would it make her not to choose her son? So much of Mary was wrapped up in being the best mother she could be for 20 years. How could she just stop?

Her attorney made it clear that she would have to do something. She could only think of questions. She could not formulate answers. The questions spun in her head until they blurred and hummed with the wind to ease her into sleep.

Safe in bed

Slowly climbing the stairs of her home, she felt the meeting with her son's attorney drain everything from her. Take the life from her. She had no more to reflect in any mirror. Vaporized and taken by the wind.

The guardian, in their brief meeting, announced his intention to follow "the wishes of the child." All the family history was irrelevant. Toby clearly stated his wish to his attorney. His wish was to live with his dad. His reason : "it is more fun at dad's." This reason was good enough for the courts. It seemed that no one had time to look at WHY it was so much more fun.

The attorney admitted that he did not read any of the documents Mary sent to him. Documents like counselors reports to the court, court orders, school records. All irrelevant. Mary left the meeting feeling dizzy and irrelevant.

"When you cannot focus, just begin. By beginning, you jettison yourself into focus." She could not remember when she had written those words. Trying to clear her mind was like trying to see the sky through the trees. Had she written those words before, or just now? It didn't matter. The fact was, she did not have the energy to begin anything.

She unplugged the phone to insure her stasis. She walked herself through the paces of locking up the house in her mind. Yes, she had double locked every door and set the alarm. She was safe, and out of the wind, the air, the commotion. Now all she could do was pray for this moment to end, and the next one, to not begin. She briefly imagined a tornado picking her house up, and ending her life. Crawling back under the bed covers, she drew the comforter over her head and fell back to sleep.

Goodbye Pat

All right, she can do this. After watching Opra's TV
show on facing your fears, she decided to have a little talk
with Pat. Of course, it wasn't really Pat. She knew that
Pat could never come close to being able to handle this
much of her. Pat had drawn a huge circle around herself
and made it very clear that entry was not possible long
ago.

Today, through her tears, she decided to reinvent Pat to
try and let go of the emotions keeping her prisoner. She
picked up the big red Clifford off the overstuffed chair in
her room and pinned a photograph of Pat to him. She
then grabbed her rocker and faced it toward the effigy.
Sitting down, she slowly began to rock.

What was it that she needed to tell Pat? Pat, who had
become closer to her than either of her blood sisters after
marrying her brother Shawn. Pat, who had continued to
reach out to her for closeness in the family until closeness
did not suit her anymore. Pat, who relied on her when
her marriage to Shawn was rocky, calling everyday. Mary
had spoken to both of them everyday for weeks, talking
Shawn into trying a recovery program for alcoholism to
save his marriage. What was it about Pat that she could
not let go of?

She got up and fluffed Clifford a bit in her chair. Sitting
again, she rocked furiously. "Why does it hurt so much
that YOU turned your back on me?" After all, everyone
else in the family had done the same. Why did she expect
Pat to be any different?

What a neive fantasy of family she had. One that
included closeness, sharing, support, caring. It wasn't that
she expected her family to be perfect. They had already

seen terrible times. When did it start falling apart? They were there for each other's weddings, the birth of 14 grandchildren…Somewhere, in mid life, after all their own children were born, family values like loyalty, history, support, friendship lost importance. Shouldn't the opposite have happened? It seemed to Mary that here in mid-life, her brothers and sisters needed each other the most. Somehow, a few years before her divorce when she lost touch because of her own problems, that closeness disappeared. Or was it gone only for her? Maybe it was only Mary that was lost to the family.

"Well Pat, I tried everything I could think of to get you to understand what was happening to me once I filed for divorce. The violence and abuse - financial, emotional, psychological, physical. Did I tell you about the way he stares in public? The way he expresses contempt every chance he gets? Well, I guess you saw that for yourself at mom's wake. Or were you even paying attention, did you even care? Why couldn't any of you tell him to go? Why did you tell him it was alright to come, even though I had explained that he had just been arrested for violence on my doorstep? Do you think ignoring it makes it easier? Are you all that sick?"

"I don't know why I expected you to be different Pat. Maybe because you were one of the only people in the family who could see the cancer of alcoholism eating away at us. You were one of the few people to join me in an effort to recognize it and keep the family together. Or maybe I just assumed that you wanted to keep the family together. Maybe your only intention was to keep your husband and children together. How is it you can understand the threat that alcohol makes to a family, and not the threat that violence presents? How could you stand by and watch me and my children suffer? I thought you loved me like I loved you. I thought I could count on your love and support. Guess not."

"I grew up thinking that being different in my family, a fact that I was constantly reminded of, was alright. I thought I could use my differences as strengths and provide leadership, bring insight. I helped everyone else through their pain. Until the family turned their backs on mine. Why did YOU? I felt that you understood me better than anyone, that we had a sisterhood in that understanding. But I guess you didn't care enough to understand me. Funny how all those years I thought you did. Maybe I just needed to think that. Because the pain in knowing that it isn't true, that NO ONE in my family cares enough to love and support me must have been too much to bear then. I think it still is."

She felt her face wet with tears and the stillness of her body. The rocking had stopped. She sat, lost and drained. Strong hard wind rattled the windows. When she opened her eyes the sun had set and the room was dark. She looked across the room to the mirror that reflected only darkness. She searched her mind to remember the day and time. Her mouth was dry and her throat nearly closed from thirst. As her eyes adjusted to the darkness she saw Clifford nestled in the chair across from her, a picture on his side. What was that picture, love, pain, emptiness, abandonment, connection, history? It is whatever you bring to it. She found that she could not stand to bring. Exhausted, she fell back to sleep.

Goodbye Toby

She moved around a bit in her chair to get comfortable, to find her center. Then she continued.

"Please let the judge know that I have serious concerns about the environment at his father's home and the effect it will have on him if he lives there full time. There are no rules, he comes and goes as he pleases without accountability. He is left alone for long periods of time without supervision. His father's alcoholism makes availability of alcohol an issue. His school attendance during his dad's visitation periods was always an issue as are his study habits while there. Not to mention the violent behavior of the now full time role model."

"My X has not paid income tax for years! His income is psoriatic and unreliable. He has been evicted from 4 homes in the last 6 years. This has all been overlooked by the court. Don't they think it will limit my son's future?"

"Toby doesn't understand now, how this will limit his future. He is just thinking about the really fast classic car his dad has given him, the incredible amount of money that his father gives him and the fact that anything goes over there. If you were a 15 year old boy, what would you choose? Well, these are the wishes of the child. Who did not see that coming when they set the trend in family court?"

"My son's attorney strictly follows the current trends of the court. By doing this, he serves his own political position and not my son's best interests. During the divorce, the trend was "Joint Legal Custody," which he recommended to the court with disastrous results. It set the stage for years of domestic violence to follow."

"The current trend is to follow the "wishes of the child" instead of the "best interest of the child." He recommends doing this while ignoring all of the alienation, the court order violations, the dangerous and illegal behavior of the father. He ignores all of the psychological reports that tell the court that the relationship between father and son is destructive to the son because of the father's psychological domination and the son's co-dependence. He ignores those reports that tell of my son's need for structure and the absence of structure in his father's environment."

"I spent all I can and gave the court everything it needs to make a decision that is in the best interest of the child. To continue now would mean financial ruin for me."

"In this county - only the rich can get support from family court. Not many single moms are in that position today."

"I have spent countless days in every courtroom in that courthouse over the years, listening to stories of children attempting suicide or parents attempting suicide. Does the court see any responsibility here? When you assign a family with a history of abuse Joint Legal Custody, you set the scene for the abuse to intensify. When you tell a teenager he can choose between his parents when the family has a history of abuse and alienation, you set the stage for the unspeakable. Is it the laws that are outdated? Is it the people that are applying the laws that do not have the time to listen? Can't the court see that it overburdens itself by not taking the time to make the changes needed to be effective? Family court is failing families. Does anyone care?"

"When you filed my first motion thirteen months ago, my son was happily living with me. My X's response to my filing to recoup child support was intensified alienation tactics. The court did nothing to stop this."

"When this began, I got a $1000 loan for a retainer. You told me that you would return the retainer to me once he was court ordered to pay your fees. But his fight back response was exacerbated by the court instead of suppressed. One issue after another put up for status week after week and never resolved, including taking my son out of state for a week during the school year. This is just one example of his violating the parenting agreement to bait me into court action. Just one example of a successful tool for alienation. That's just one - you know there are many more."

"And the result of all of this alienation in the absence of any support for me from the court is that my son is now not speaking to me and refuses to see me. Six weeks and another $1000 ago, Toby's attorney stated that the goal here is to restore the relationship between mother and child. I have not gotten a call from this attorney and I have not been able to convince my son to come and see me. Doesn't any one think this is odd? Why refuse to see me even though, according to the child's attorney, the only reason my son does not want to live with me is because he has more fun at his dad's house? Apparently, no one cares enough to look carefully at the pieces of this puzzle. No one cares enough about my son to take more than five minutes to think about this case when it is before them, until they schedule the next status hearing so they can put off thinking about it again."

"The judge is so tired of this case that he insists my X and I not be present in court. He does not want to see my tears or hear his lies. Imagine that."

"I have two sons. I cannot risk the future of one for the sake of the other. If Toby truly understands that the court believes it is following his wishes, then he will need to take a stand. I need to love him enough to let him go. He will need enough room to figure this out for himself. Will he be able to if he is using alcohol and other drugs? I don't know. I told his attorney about the beer and drug paraphernalia that I found in his room. But apparently, I am the only one who cares, and I am powerless."

"What I want you to do now is request a status date toward the end of the school year. Let's give Toby all the room he needs to figure this out.."

"No!" the attorney injected. "I think we should get a date before Christmas. Don't you want him home for the holidays?"

Mary's rant had created a powerful thirst. She took a long drink of water before she continued.

"He will come home when he is ready. If the court is unwilling to enforce the parenting agreement, nothing I can do will persuade him if he isn't ready. Apparently, the decision needs to be his. If he wants to be here for the holidays, he will be. We don't need a court date for that."

"If, in April, he has not returned home, I will agree to amend the parenting agreement and pay child support. This is a moral choice for me. If he is not with me, I need to be contributing financially to his care. I want the judge to know that."

"I love my son. No one can take that away. Not from me. Not from Toby. Not the courts. Not my X. No one. If my son needs to leave me to get some well deserved peace in his life, and we cannot give him other options, then I need to love him enough to let him go. And I do. With all my broken heart, I do."

"Mary, I am so sorry."

Mary whispered, "me too. Thank you."

With that, she hung up the phone and took a long deep breath. She stared hard at the print of Georgia O'Keefe's White Rose that hung on her wall across from her. She got all caught up in the swirl of white and blue and lost herself for awhile.

I am in an enclosed porch looking out into a large yard. The porch is enclosed in glass and I am afraid that an earthquake will shatter the glass around me.

I see Toby in the yard. The glass blurs his image. He begins to walk toward me. The closer he gets, the more I can see bugs hopping and flying around him. When he gets half way through the yard I can see that the bugs are grasshoppers. Some have landed on him.

I take my eyes off of Toby because I notice a severed head laying on the floor in a corner of the porch. Terrified, I run out of the room and the dream ends.

Torn

Walking back to the townhouse, Mary flipped through the mail. The sun was bright. Her eyes were still trying to adjust through the tears. She cried all morning. No single reason. Her world was simply full of tears that needed to spill over. Alone, she cried through the dark silence of the night into the morning. And now in an effort to pull out of it, she dressed and walked outside to get the mail. Her puffy eyes felt a sting from the sun's brilliance.

As she focused on a letter from her attorney, her feet stopped. Her mind screamed. That familiar, silent scream that filled her entire being. That paralyzed her. She had a brief, sudden wish that a truck would run her over. End the pain.

Sitting on the curb, she slowly opened the letter. It was a court summons. Her X had officially filed for custody of her youngest son. Her breath left her body as if punched out. Numbness and disbelief overwhelmed her. She closed her eyes and tried to find herself. All emptiness. And tears.

Opening her eyes, she slowly picked up her mail and somehow found the energy needed to walk home.

In order

When the files on her lap slipped to the floor, she did not move to recover them right away. Her mind was far away from her body, that was sitting in the living room chair as the evening light faded from the room.

As mind found body again, a tree outside her window came into focus and she watched the leaves fall, slowly gliding to the ground. With a sigh, she leaned over to pick up the files. It was impossible to keep her mind focused lately. So many emotions cluttered it. So many memories took control of time. Here and now came and went without effort.

She put the files in alphabetical order. She needed to make sure that everything was in order and easy for C. Jay to understand. He seemed startled when she mentioned that she had written a will. Actually, she had implemented a living trust, with everything in his name also. It would all become his without too much trouble. What little she had to leave the boys was all documented in a few files that sat on her lap. A few stocks, insurance policies, mortgage papers, trust accounts, auto documents would transfer to her children without debt. She placed her attorney's file on top and began to staple cards inside the cover of the file: accountant, broker, etc.

How amazing that her life's documentation could be held in a handful of files. One of the files held her copyrights. The actually writing itself was stored in boxes in the garage. Along with childhood treasures from the boys growing up years. Along with picture albums. While putting her life in order, she made sure everything was organized and stored. If the boys decided to keep the townhouse, they probably wouldn't find most of it until they decided to move.

She sat up and tried to shake the future fantasy out of her head. Just another stray thought to send on its way.

As she climbed the stairs, she looked at each of the pictures that hung on the stairway wall. A pictorial history of the family including parents, grandparents, siblings, children had grown over the years. A new historian would need to carry it on. At the top of the stairs, she gasped for breath and clenched her chest to feel her breaking heart. She was tired, much too tired.

After placing the files in the C. Jay's file drawer along with his own bank account and college financing information, she went into her bedroom to lay down. Darkness descended and the house felt cold. Covering herself with a blanket, she was asleep before her mind could wander elsewhere.

"Hello," came out of Mary as a whisper.

"Mary, did I wake you? It is two in the afternoon. Are you alright? I left a message for you at work, but thought I would also try you at home. I am glad I found you. I'm worried about you because I didn't hear from you about the motion to modify custody. You usually call me as soon as you receive a motion with so much to say. Are you alright?"

Mary could hear the serious concern in her attorney's voice. Yesterday, she may have felt compelled to say something comforting, to put her mind at ease. Today, Mary only felt a powerful thirst, and a terrible pain in her heart that kept her from feeling compassion for others and herself. As she reached for her glass of water, she took a deep breath.

"Are you there Mary?" her attorney asked.

After a drink of water, Mary answered, "Where else could I be? Yes, I am here. Although honestly, I don't know where here is any more. We both know that if this judge and Toby's attorney had any desire to send Toby back to me, they would have done so months ago. Now, Toby has been completely alienated from me and saying he wants to live with his dad. His father has successfully talked him into abandoning me. And although I tried everything I could think of, accessed every available resource, I could not prevent it because the court did nothing to stop it. They knew it was going on and did nothing. Why do they bother to put language about alienation in the joint parenting agreement if no one intends to do anything about it? I feel like everyone just sits back and watches my life shatter and says, 'Oh well, too bad. Nothing we can do.'"

Mary took another drink of water while her attorney responded, "Mary, it is not that we don't care. He is Toby's father. Toby is old enough to decide what his wishes are. That is just the way it is."

"Oh come on." Mary was getting angry now. "Court order after court order was violated and he was not once found in contempt. All each judge did was scheduling another court date. Waiting for more information I suppose. What the hell happens to all of those unanswered motions, floating around in court space? Hasn't paid the children's expenses. Taken them out of state without consent. Not bringing them home according to the schedule. The alienation. The harassment. All of that was overlooked. Do the courts have any idea about how all of that effects a family? The psychological development of the children? The mental health of a person who can do nothing to prevent it and gets no support from the court to stop it? I am completely defeated. I feel utterly hopeless. Sometimes, I don't think I can make it through the day. This next court date is just a formality. The judge still probably does not even want me in the court room again. So that he does not have to look at the devastating effects of his indecision."

"Mary I am so sorry. I know that you are angry. But you need to pull yourself together. That is why I am calling. You need to present yourself as someone capable of having custody. I am still hoping that this judge will see how unhealthy it is over at your X's. He won't see that if he sees you falling apart."

"Funny, I started this process a perfectly capable parent. President of the local parent network. Teaching parenting classes to my neighbors. Working with the children in my community to enhance their moral code. Now look at me. I can't even get out of bed and look in the mirror. And I don't want to."

"Mary listen, our court appearance is next Friday. You need to pull yourself together. Talk to a counselor if you need to. Call me by Wednesday if you don't feel that you can do this, and I will get a continuance. But sooner or later, you will need to face this. Please, call me if you need help."

"Yea, sure, why not," Mary said as she hung up. Burrowing under the covers, she hummed herself to sleep.

I watch, a woman who is me, as if I am watching a movie.

She sits, nestled in the roots of the tree, resting against the enduring trunk. She moves her feet in the river water, stares at the harvest moonlight and inspires the sweet autumn air with a smile. Happily, she hums the tune of the church bell symphony carried in her heart since childhood.

As the wind picks up, it takes her breath away and she retreats to her car for shelter. Before leaving, she adjusts her seat and mirror and takes one last mental picture of her beloved river bank and her climbing tree.

Driving through the cold, darkness and silence, a terrific thirst overtakes her and she screams to end it. And then whispers, "my love."

I can't seem to get rid of a terrible headache so please pardon any incoherence. I haven't heard from you in so long and really need to connect. I feel so unconnected lately, disconnected, numb really.

I had a kind of out of body experience yesterday that has not let go of me. I was sitting in the court house, waiting for the inevitable verdict that my X will get custody of Toby. I tried to listen to all of the activity around me. Many people on cell phones, reliving their stories, most angry. All kinds of people, dirty, well dressed, handsome, ugly, kind, aggressive. All talking or listening. I tried to see and listen to all of it at once but it was just too much. I stopped trying.

Suddenly, I WAS able to see and hear and understand it all at once. And once I was able to do that, I understood that all of those people were a part of me. No matter how repulsive or attractive, they were all a part of me. The more repulsive, the more they reflected my negativity. It was my own busy mirror.

This frightened me because some of these people were very repulsive, potentially violent and abusive. I was in the courthouse after all. But I had to let go of my fright to maintain this level of consciousness. If I felt emotion, I began to focus and lose my ability to understand it all.

What brought me to the courthouse was the fact that Bob has finally succeeded in alienating Toby from me. Nothing and no one was able to stop that, although everyone knew that it was happening all of these years. The court considers Toby old enough to be able to decide that he does not want me in his life. I know, that he tells people this to please his dad, and hang on to the classic

drag racer that was his 15th birthday present from his dad.
He thinks that I will always be there and that I am strong
enough to handle this. He thinks that he needs to take
care of his dad, not the other way around. And even
though the court knows all of this, they will allow it.
Heartbreaking.

Today, the court awarded custody of Toby to his father.
I can't believe it.

Toby tells me he loves me and that he will be home soon.
If he believes this, he is in for his own heartbreak,
because his father will never allow it. His need to
dominate Toby has become all consuming.

I wondered if I created the reality that brought me to the
courthouse. Bob and all his crazy behavior. Toby's
rejection of me. In the courthouse, I didn't feel like they
were effected by me. I felt like they WERE me and living
to express a part of me. I wondered if my aversion of
what I judged to be negative created the negativity. If my
aversion brought more negativity into my life.

I felt myself tear in two with an actual, physical pain that
runs from my head through my breaking heart.. I
somehow not only lost the will to engage in the
courtroom drama, but to engage in life. I knew, that
wherever I went, and whoever was around me would only
be a reflection of who I was. I don't recognize this
reflection anymore.

This means that the trouble with the down turning
economy, my financial troubles, the war in the middle
east and international terrorism, not to mention Bob's
terrorism since the divorce are all just a reflection of my
will.

But I do not know how to change it for the better. I don't know what to "do." After listening to all the advisors, thought I made the best decisions possible, based on my values and the best interest of my children. But I feel like such a failure.

And I wonder why I would will myself to be completely alone. C. Jay and Toby now gone. My family distant. No real ties, no real connection. Why would I create this reality when what I think I want is the opposite? How do I turn it around?

Now part of me remains connected/disconnected. And part of me is pure pain. Both parts ring together like church bells, the sound of my soul's longing.

I don't know where to go from here so I will take another pain pill.

I still wonder about the meaning of our "cross to bear." Is our cross those parts of ourselves that create pain, that we don't understand, that are opposite of our personal best, our aversions? How do we prevent our own crucifixion? Can we prevent it?

I think that I made many mistakes. That I did not see the signs before me. I think that these mistakes became my cross. I thought, that if I did my best in the face of adversity, I would live a life close to god, a life with joy. I thought that everyday, I did my best. I thought that if I loved my children with my whole heart, and tried every day to be the best mother I could be, our love would prevail.

I must have been wrong. Because now I feel it all slipping away: my home, my family, my life.

All I know now, is that my head aches with the wondering. My spirit is numb, and my body is wracked with pain. Each moment, I wait for the pain to end, but it doesn't, so I take another pill.

I can hardly whisper, "It is all part of my own reflection. A distorted mirror. A distant life. A divided me. Slipping away."

Many thanks, for a lifetime of love and inspiration. With my final breath I thank you and I love you. From soul to body. Forever in my heart.

mmb

Separate peace

She sat cross legged on a small cloud. Somewhere within, her soul composed and orchestrated music simultaneously. Listening carefully, she could find a single emotion within each note. All pieces of the orchestra played endlessly the music that was her.

Surrounding her, simultaneous realities - people, places, things, color, light, shadows that have and will touch her. Nothing good or bad, no pain or joy. Simply experience. Without desire. Such power in keeping the music separate from the reality, such peace.

Before her, from her, white light lit an endless path. A path that opened up and drew her in. That became her, that she became. The farther she followed the path, the more reality slipped away. And peace became her. And she became peace.

It's C. Jay. I'm alone now. I don't know where you are. For the first time in my life, I don't know where you are. I don't know if you have forgotten me. And I need to feel you here with me. I really miss you mom. But I know that you are gone forever. Will you remember me?

I'm writing this letter because it is the only way I can talk to you now. I remember how you would write me letters and say all kinds of stuff that you wanted me to know. Mom stuff. Stuff about doing the right thing and believing and knowing who I am. Now I don't know if I will ever know who I am without you. I've never written this kind of letter before. I'm writing this letter because I don't know what else to do.

All these years you have been writing me letters and I did not write one letter to you. I don't know why. I guess I always felt before that you would be there for me to talk to when I needed you. And I never really understood why you wrote those letters to me. I hope I did not seem too ungrateful, because now it seems like all I have left of you. The real you. The you I could turn to, the voice that I knew deep in my heart. Your voice calmed me down and made me happy as soon as I heard it. You left me that voice in your letters. Did you know you would be leaving so soon? God I wish you were still here. My life will never be as good without you.

I wanted to share my future with you. I never imagined that you wouldn't be there to tell me how proud you were, the way you always did. How will I know that I am on the right track now? You were the only person in this world that I had to turn to, Mom. How could you take that away?

I always hated it when I would sigh, and you knew what was bothering me. All I had to do was sigh. And I didn't even do it on purpose. I always thought that was so annoying, the way you seemed to know my thoughts and feelings. But I didn't understand that connection to you, how it filled me with love and courage to do my best every day because that's what you wanted. That connection made me feel that someone cared about every breath I took, every one of my feelings. It made me feel valuable in this world. How will I feel that now? I just now understand that no one else shows me my value like you did. No one ever will. I feel so sad and empty.

You were the one person in this world that I could count on to guide me in the right direction, the one person I always believed. I didn't ever really mind when you would panic or over react to things. I knew a hug or simple I love you would calm you down. Even having the power to calm you and help you made me strong. I won't have that strength without you. I won't be the same.

I'm so sorry now about all the stuff I made you do. Laundry, cooking, paperwork, even paying for things. Maybe if I had done more myself you would still be here. Maybe if I cleaned up more and helped you more. Maybe if I had kept dad away from you more, not told him to come over to pick me up or give me things. Maybe if I had protected you more. God, I wish I helped you more. I want to take it all back and start over. I promise I will be better this time if you only come back. Please come back. I will tell you I love you every day and help you every day. Please.

If you come back I won't make fun of you for knowing who I was with before I got home. Like that time I got a ticket driving my car and you already knew before I told you. I hated that people were watching and telling you everything. But now I miss that because it means that no one is there for me. It feels like no one cares.

I never told you I didn't like it when you said "have a good day, do your very best, and don't forget I love you" every day when I left for school. Every damn day. And your "treat everyone with respect and kindness" thing. I thought it was so dumb. Now I miss it.

I won't have a mom making friends with the football coach (and his wife) at the games and dinners. I won't hear your voice cheering or yelling. I wish I had not been so embarrassed by that. Or by the hugs you wanted when I came off the field. Or by the fact that you were always waiting for me after the games outside the locker rooms, usually talking to a teacher or coach or player. I hated that you were telling them things and finding out things about me. I don't hate it any more. I will be so sad every time I come away from a game and you aren't there. Just to see your smile first thing. And to hear you remind me of all the good things I did on the field. I'd give anything to get that back.

I watched that high school football highlights tape that you helped me make for the college recruiters. I remembered all the hours we spent watching my high school football game tapes. And how you made me mad because you wanted to include every play that I touched the ball, whether it was a good run or not. But now I remember how the guy from the Yale home visit said that it was a better highlights tape than Yale makes! And how proud I was of you then. I want to be proud of you again just like that. I don't want to just have to remember it. I need you to be real in my life, not just a memory.

I probably sound like a big baby here, and you know I'm really a tough guy. The thing is that you are the only person who would understand this baby babble. And you would tell me it's OK to feel like this. You would help me through it and hold me. You wouldn't tell me to be tough or that it was all up to me now. I don't want it to be all up to me. I thought we were good partners. I held you sometimes when you cried. And you hugged me every day. We talked about stuff that disappointed us. Didn't I make you happy enough? Why couldn't my love stop you?

I feel so mad that you left me alone. But I'm afraid that my anger will hurt you still. So now I'm both mad and afraid and that sucks. I can't explain it to anyone. I hit someone the other day. I never did that before. It happened before I knew what I was doing. Poor guy just made a stupid joke. He never saw it coming. The coach called me into his office and I didn't know what to say. When he asked what you would think about it, I had to tell him that you died. Then I don't think he knew what to say. He just said he will miss the way you smiled when you looked at me. I guess he didn't realize that just hurt more. Because now I know that I will miss that too.

I was just beginning to see you as a person. I wish I could have seen all of your pain. Then maybe I could have done something to stop it. I wish I had never gone away to college. If you needed me so much, why did you tell me to go? You said that you were so happy for me. Why couldn't you be happy for yourself? At least until I got back home. Then I would have helped you. I would give anything to be able to help you now.

You used to tell me that my voice in my writing was a lot like yours. I never knew what you meant until now. I read your letters over and over and it is like you are still here with me. I can hear your voice again. Saying the words in the letters and even saying other stuff that you would say after I read them. When I think I have forgotten the sound of your voice, I read some letters and it comes back to me. Right out of my heart.

I want you to know that I will keep your voice with me always. And I will keep doing my best so that I can tell myself that you are proud of me. I will hear your voice saying it. And I will share your voice with my children for you. And they will share it with their children. Because life goes on even though you aren't here. It just hurts a lot more.

Dear C. Jay,

Because you are reading this letter, it means that I am gone and you are doing just as I asked you to do afterward. Thank you. This folder contains the things I put into place for you to make the financial and physical transition easier.

I have tried, over the years, to give you all the best advice that I could find, all the best info. I worked as hard as I could to give you the best start that I could. And although I would have given you much more had it been in my power, I hope you take what I was able to give and use it wisely to build a strong and decent future for you and your family.

I am sorry that my time with you was so short. My heart will always be with you. And I am sure that we will be together again. We are bound, soul to soul, forever. This is one of my greatest blessings.

Please take care of Toby and stay close to him, as close as you can. Give him the advice that I gave you but did not have the chance or time to give him. Be the best older brother that you can be. He needs you.

Take the file that I showed you with my will and financial information to my attorney. Her card is in the file. There are also some additional resources listed in the file for you, financial advisors, bankers, book keepers, tax consultants. Don't be afraid to seek the help you need.

Uncle Shawn and Aunt Pat are designated as the guardians of Toby's share of the estate until he is 21. Help him use this money wisely, not wastefully afterward.

Since Toby decided to stay with dad, I had time to write again. If my book has not yet been published, take my black leather binder to Debra. The disks in it contain the entire novel. If anyone can get it published, Debra can. I think that it is an important story, and will help a lot of people. My attorney will help you with any income and royalties that this book produces for my estate. You will need to make sure that any checks are made out to the living trust that we share. I truly hope that my story provides a good financial foundation for your future. One that I could not provide while I was living. One that I could not live long enough to provide.

Discuss this book only with Debra and our attorney before it is published. No one else needs to know about the book until then. I don't want anyone to prevent you from getting it published. Just turn it over to Debra and she will work with our attorney. You need do nothing else but work with the attorney to manage the estate I leave behind that will include the income from this book.

Don't put off doing what you need to do financially. You need to settle the estate and file taxes yearly from now on. Make sure you do. Some of your teachers or coaches may have good advice for you. You are now the head of the family. Plan and implement a bright future for yourself. Surround yourself with successful people who can give you support and advice.

Please forgive me for leaving you so soon. I would have stayed with you longer if I had the choice. I will be with you forever, in a different way. Just look in your heart when you are quiet. I will be there to guide you, whispering I love you when you need to hear it. I wasn't strong enough to stay longer, but our love is strong enough to last your whole life. Let it guide you when you become a parent, when you are finding your faith, when you love your wife and family. If you love them with your whole heart, the way you loved me, your love will last.

You are an excellent person. A splendid spirit. A strong man. Please don't ever loose sight of that. Even when life is difficult and you don't feel like you can do enough....believe that you are all these things and life will improve with time. Remember who you are, my bright and beautiful son.

Your love means everything to me. It has become the heart of my soul, and I take it with me, to guide me to you. I know that wherever I am, you are with me, your love will fill me.

I love you always, and will always be with you.

Your mom

Dear Toby,

I hope that you will read this letter after it is given to you and it will help to remind you that I love you with my whole heart. You may wonder how that is possible because you are angry that I left you. You may have blamed lots of different people, including yourself. I want you to know this important fact: MY DEATH WAS NOT ANYONE'S FAULT. No one is to blame, especially you. Please believe me, it is very true.

I was just born without much strength. Like I was born with asthma and allergies. Like a person born that cannot walk. Or a person born that cannot see. You would not blame those people because they couldn't do those things. And you would not blame yourself. Please understand. And know that although my heart broke many times in my life, you did not break it. You gave me some challenging moments as a mom. And so did your brother. But good moms are always challenged to be better. So thank you.

You may be remembering the rough time we had during my divorce from your father. You said and did things to express your pain. You may regret some of these now. Please have no regrets about this. I understood even then that you were working things out in your own way, doing what you had to so that your broken heart would mend. And I admired you for that. You became my hero. You tried so hard. I am proud of you for being able to do that. It takes great strength and courage and you did it. You lived through that rough time and still loved me and dad and C. Jay and lots of other people in your life. You are awesome. And you will always be my hero.

Please do not let the tragedy of my life effect yours. Leave my tragedy behind and take with you only the joy we shared. Remember my life's great moments. My smile, embrace, comfort. You brought joy to my life from the moment you entered it, a perfect, cuddly, brilliant baby. You are a splendid person. Your splendor has always shown and filled those around you with warmth and love and hope. Don't ever let pain get in the way of knowing this splendor inside you, your bright spirit. It is genuine and real.

Try to remember the things that I told you about strength of character and the importance of family. Someday, you will marry and have children of your own. Treat your wife and children like rare jewels. Treat them with complete respect at all times. It is not always easy, but it is necessary for keeping the family together. Listen closely to them. Listening is much more important that being heard. I am so sorry if I wasn't a good listener. I tried, but maybe the pain in my heart blocked my ability to really listen. Don't let that happen to you.

Life is difficult and sometimes painful. Accept that. Use it to strengthen character. Find a way to leave your pain behind you. Strong people do that. You can do that. I believe that you and your brother are both very strong inside. Keep up the good work and find ways every day to strengthen your character, the way you strengthen your body and your mind.

All teenagers try on deception, rebellion, defiance. It is the job of a teenager to try these on and discover who they are and who they do not want to become. To become a strong man you will need to discover that deception, rebellion and defiance destroy love, break trust, take opportunity from you, weaken character. They are self destructive behaviors. You will need to leave these behaviors behind to become a man of strong character. Please do this for me. I know you can. Try instead truth, teamwork, cooperation and community.

Never forget, your character is your fate. A good, strong character will have a good, strong fate.

I believe that you truly want to find deep, abiding love. Love is an action. By acting with honesty, respect, kindness, compassion and hard work will bring love to strengthen your character. Look at the values we talked every New Year's Eve about and bring them into your life. They will strengthen your character. They will bring you happiness.

I believe that when I die I will be able to watch over you. I might be able to reach you in a dream. Or talk to you through your conscience. But most of all I believe that I will see you again, in heaven or another life or whatever comes after this life. I believe that we love each other so much, that we are bound together forever. Where I am now, my pain has stopped. Please use my love and all of the things that I tried to teach you to minimize your own pain in this world. I will be waiting for you in the next.

Love forever,

Your mom